UNSILENT GRIEF

TONY MILLINGTON

Copyright © 2018 by Tony Millington

All rights reserved.
Published in 2018 by: Britain's Next Bestseller
An imprint of Live It Ventures LTD
27 Old Gloucester Road,
London.
WC1N 3AX
www.bnbsbooks.co.uk

The moral right of Tony Millington to be identified as the author of this work has been asserted by him in accordance with the Copyright, Designs and Patents Act 1988.
Except as permitted under current legislation, no part of this work may be photocopied, stored in a retrieval system, published, performed in public, adapted, broadcast, transmitted, recorded or reproduced in any form or by any means, without the prior permission of the copyright owners.
All enquiries should be addressed to:
Live It Ventures LTD,

Cover design by Joe O'Connell

Printed in the U.K

ISBN - 978-1-910565-38-4

This book is dedicated to my beautiful wife Ann and my amazing son Richard who are my rocks.

1

TUESDAY EVENING, 11.30P.M.

RONALD FREEMAN DOWNED the dregs of his final pint and said goodnight to the landlord of his local pub, The Dragon's Den.

He'd been cheering on their pool team, who had beaten The King's Head 7-2 in the local league. The last to leave having consumed far too much alcohol, he staggered through the back door of the pub towards the car park. He zig-zagged across the potholes in the tarmac, trying to avoid tripping over them, towards his car. It had been raining most of the evening, so the holes were full of water.

He lit his last cigarette and threw the empty packet on the ground. As he reached the car door, he fumbled for the keys in his trousers pocket, dropping them on the floor, and muttering under his breath. He leaned down and grabbed them before opening the door of the battered silver VW Passat, which was parked haphazardly next to a wall at the back of the carpark.

Freeman slid into the driver's seat and started the engine, doing the seatbelt up, with the cigarette hanging from his mouth. There was a sharp knock on the driver's window. Puzzled, he wound the window down and glared through the cigarette smoke and beer haze to see a human form standing by his car.

"Mr. Ronald Freeman?" the stranger asked him.

"Yes? And who the fuck wants to know?" Freeman snarled back.

"This is for Fredrick Mason," Colin Littlewood calmly said. With that he fired twice into the car.

The back of Freemans's head exploded as the bullets entered through the forehead, showering the inside of the car with pieces of skull and brain matter. He slumped in the seat, being held in place only by his seat belt.

Littlewood stuffed his gun into the deep pocket of his donkey jacket and disappeared into the shadows.

———

COLIN LITTLEWOOD KNEW WHERE FREEMAN WOULD BE that night.

Having watched him for over a week, Colin had followed him at a safe distance whilst working out the best time and place to kill him. He discovered the security light did not reach the back corners of the car park, an excellent place to wait in the shadows near the industrial sized bins. It was the ideal place to put a bullet in his head without being noticed. Unfortunately, as he waited he had to endure the terrible smell of the pub waste in the bins, but the result was worth it.

As Littlewood slipped away unnoticed, he wished he had chosen a different coat to wear that night. The donkey jacket was heavy after the latest torrential downpour.

Littlewood thought back to the events of the evening.

Most of Freeman's visits to the Dragon's Den ended up with him leaving completely hammered. How he could drive in that state, without getting pulled over, was a mystery to Littlewood. He had watched Freeman say goodnight to the landlord as he was locking up. Freeman had then staggered all the way to the car, trying to light a cigarette. When he had managed to open the car, and get inside, Littlewood had made his move. He had slowly walked towards the vehicle, not letting Freeman see him until it was too late to do anything.

After a brief exchange of words, he had put two bullets into that scumbag's head. He had then calmly walked through the back gate at the far end of the car park and into the darkness. He had checked around to ensure that nobody had seen a thing.

Walking away at his normal pace, feeling euphoric he said to himself, "One down." He smiled!

Revenge was sweet.

TERRY WATSON WAS TURNING OFF THE LIGHTS AND GETTING ready for bed, when the 'War of the Worlds' theme music blared from his phone.

His wife Sally scowled; first at the clock which read midnight and then back at him. "Who could be ringing at this time of night?" she asked sarcastically, sighing because she already knew the answer.

Terry thought about cracking a joke but decided now was not the best time. He picked up the phone from the bedside table. "Watson?"

"I'll be outside in five," Keith Monteith announced as he flung himself into the driver's seat of his two-year-old blue BMW 1 series. Keith was Terry's partner-in-crime, or crime prevention, as they occasionally joked.

"Where's the fire?"

"No fire! It was a shooting," Monteith responded, as he started the engine.

"I'll be waiting." Watson heard the car wheels spin as Monteith pulled away and disconnected from the hands-free.

Watson quickly threw on a pair of jeans, socks and a clean shirt, as Sally looked on. He checked he had everything including his police I.D, warrant card, and radio. Then he unlocked the wall safe and reached in for his gun.

"Do you have to go?" Sally said nervously as she got out of bed wearing just a white t-shirt with Bugs Bunny on it.

She hated when he had to rush off to a call where a serious crime had been committed. She dreaded to think what kind of risk he was at. What if one day she got the call, or the visit, that every wife feared? The one that meant he wouldn't be coming home? She followed him out of the bedroom as he pulled on his leather jacket.

"After fifteen years of marriage you still ask me that." Watson turned when he reached the top of the stairs and kissed her.

"Yes, because I care, you silly sod." Sally sighed loudly, taking one last cuddle and kiss before he started to walk down the stairs.

"Love you Sally," he called as he opened the front door.

"Love you too, darling." She watched him disappear and slam the door.

"Where's Daddy going?" A tired voice called out from one of the bedrooms.

Sally opened the door. Their eight-year-old daughter Rachael was sitting up in bed rubbing her eyes. "He has to go into work little miss, and you should be asleep. Did we wake you?" Sally entered the room and tucked her back into bed.

"I heard Dad's phone going off and both of you talking," Rachael said as she lay back down and rubbed her closing eyes.

"He will be back soon darling. Now I think we should both try to get some sleep." She kissed her daughter on the forehead. "Goodnight sweetie."

The little girl, half asleep, cuddled up to her favourite teddy bear dressed as a policeman. "Night Mum."

As Watson shut and locked the front door Monteith was already outside waiting. His car's headlights showed a fine rain was still falling. Watson jumped into the passenger seat.

"Got out alive then?" Monteith said, as he floored the BMW.

"Yes. Sally was fine. Wasn't Katie?"

"I think the last thing I heard her mumble beneath the duvet was piss off and save the world then," Monteith laughed.

2

MONTEITH AND WATSON had been partners in the Criminal Detective Agency of the West Ravenswood Police Force for the last five years.

West Ravenswood was a small city with a population of around 150,000. It was much like every other city or town. It had areas you would love to live, but can't afford, areas you wouldn't live even if someone paid you to, and some areas which were ok, the middle of the road areas.

The detectives had gone to school together, graduated in the same year, and then qualified for the Police Academy. After their initial two year P.C. training and Neighbourhood/Response training, they were posted to different areas of policing. When the force set up the CDA, both had made detective grade and the obvious candidates to be assigned to it.

They were even each other's best man at their weddings.

They reached the crime scene and parked up on the street in front of The Dragon's Den in the Bankside section of the city. The area had been secured with crime tape, across the gateway at the side of the pub. Floodlights illuminated the car park at the rear, reaching into the areas the security light could not. A tent was erected to cover the car from onlookers and prevent any potential for evidence contamination. Under the tent, the forensics investigators were carefully going over a VW Passat with its driver's door open.

Watson and Monteith could see the body which remained in the car. It was not a pretty sight.

Sergeant Karl Lorimer took them into the pub via the back door, along a corridor and past the toilets into the main part of the pub. It was split into two, with the bar serving both sides. One was the lounge area which was made to look like a cosy snug, with soft furnishings and low lighting. It had a well-worn patterned carpet on the floor. The walls had flowered wallpaper on them, with wall lights spaced out around the room. An open fireplace with a large wooden framed mirror took pride of place along the longest wall.

Pictures of the countryside spaced out around the walls. There were half a dozen easy armchairs around small tables, and a couple beside the fire and under the front facing window. Barstools and the normal dark wooden laminated tables and wheel backed chairs made up the rest of the seating. The restaurant and the kitchen area were through a door at the far end of the room.

The other side was a games area. It wasn't quite spit and sawdust, but not far off. There were large, dirty, cream coloured tiles on the floor, and the walls and ceiling were stained dirty nicotine yellow, remnants from when smoking was still allowed inside. On the walls were the obligatory two pictures of dressed up dogs playing pool and cards. Two large windows looked out on the street outside. Blue baize coloured pool table at the far end on the room, along with a dart board. A Wurlitzer jukebox stood next to the corridor which led out to the toilets and back door. The lighting came from three shaded lights in the ceiling and two wall lights.

The wreck of a landlord, Mr. Preston, was in the spit and sawdust side, sat at the bar, nursing a glass of whiskey.

"He's given us a name of the victim in the car," Lorimer said in a hushed tone, mindful of Mr. Preston, "But nothing else."

Watson went over to the landlord, introduced himself, and sat down on a barstool,

"What can you tell us Mr. Preston?"

"I'd just shown Ronald to the door and said good night. I locked up and then a couple of minutes later I heard two bangs."

Mr. Preston paused and gulped down the whole of the large whiskey in one.

"I thought his car was backfiring, so I unlocked and went out of the door, and saw…"

With that he collapsed in tears. His body and shoulders heaving up and down as the shock of the night hit him hard. Watson leaned over and placed a hand on his shoulder and quietly thanked him. He got up and went over to where Monteith and the Sergeant were standing near the jukebox.

"We won't get much out of him tonight," Watson said looking back at Mr. Preston. "Let's see what we can find outside."

Back out in the car park, the rain had thankfully stopped. Both tried to do a quick step around the water filled pot holes. Watson failed, and his right foot went straight into one. "Bollocks!" he shouted, shaking his foot to get most of the water off.

"Good job there were floodlights on or you would have got both feet wet!" Monteith laughed.

The police pathologist James Macintosh, or Mac the Knife as he was known, had arrived and was under the tent studying Ronald Freeman's body.

"Hi Mac, what we got?" asked Monteith.

"A bloody mess that's what," Mac answered. "Why can't killers just put the bullets into the body instead of having to blow a person's brains half out! Would make my job a lot easier. Now I will have to pick this car apart to get the rest of this head."

"But you love it, don't you Mac?" grinned Monteith, trying to make light of the situation.

"Yes, great fun trying to do a skull jigsaw," Mac said with a big grin of his own.

"The landlord said he heard two bangs," Watson interjected.

"Yes… that would cause this mess. Not sure about the caliber until we find the bullets. Will let you know when I get him back to the lab."

"Have you found any identification?"

"There's a wallet here with a driving licence belonging to Ronald Freeman." Mac handed it over in a clear evidence bag to Watson.

"That name ties in with what the landlord said. Ok Mac, seems that you have everything under control here. See you back at the station." With that they left Mac and his team doing their job.

3

Littlewood parked his car on the drive next to his daughter's.

Opened his front door of his terrace house, and with one final glance around at the street to make sure he'd not been seen; entered and locked it behind him. He put his wet donkey jacket on the hanger behind the door. Satisfied with his night's work he walked into the front room. His daughter Susan was sitting on the sofa with her legs tucked up under her watching a late night film on the television. She glanced round as he entered.

"Enjoy your evening?" she said smiling.

"Yes, very enjoyable" he replied, leaning over Susan from behind and kissing her forehead. He watched the film she had on for a couple of minutes. One Flew Over the Cuckoo's Nest. He had seen it more times than he cared to remember.

"I think I'll go up, see you in the morning, sweetheart."

Susan turned her head towards him, "Night, dad."

Littlewood removed the gun from his coat and took it upstairs to his bedroom. Opening an old wardrobe, he knelt and pulled out an old rucksack which was tucked away at the back. He put the gun deep inside. Taking out a red bound book he opened it, and with the pen attached he put a line through the first name on the list, Ronald Freeman.

DETECTIVE CHIEF INSPECTOR KENNETH CROMPTON HAD BEEN the head of the Criminal Detective Agency since its conception five years ago, with over twenty years of policing behind him.

The agency was on the fourth floor of the main Police Headquarters in the city centre. Crompton was big in stature both in build and his reputation in the police force. He had come up through the ranks as a career policeman and now was the head of the newest part of the area's force. Always called a spade a spade and did not like people bullshitting him, but there to help someone who needed it.

At 1am, he was still sat behind his large wooden desk in his glass walled office. When Watson and Monteith arrived, he waved them in as he finished speaking on the phone.

"The press office is looking for a heads up, so what have we got?" Crompton said as Watson and Monteith sat in the leather backed chairs on the other side of his desk.

Watson began. "We've just got back from the shooting at The Dragon's Den Public House. White male shot whilst sitting in his car in the pub's car park around 11.30pm last night. The landlord said after locking up he heard two loud bangs. He ran out into the car park at the back of the pub and found the man's body in his car."

"Did he know who the victim was?"

"The name he has given is the same as on the victim's driving licence. Ronald Freeman."

Crompton sat bolt upright in his chair. "What? Who?"

"The victim is Ronald Freeman," Watson repeated.

He watched as the colour drained from their DCI's face. "Are you all right, Sir?" Monteith pitched in, "You look like you've seen a ghost!"

Crompton rose out of his chair and went to his cabinet, opened the bottom drawer and pulled out a bottle of whiskey. He poured two shots and sat back down, his face ashen.

"Ronald Freeman is a blast from the past. One of my first cases as a detective." Crompton took a swig of whiskey.

"He was jailed for the manslaughter of a shop owner Fred Mason fifteen years ago. Everyone working the case said it should have been murder. He went into the place to rob it with a sawn off shotgun. Mason did not give in and tackled him. The gun went off in the struggle. Mason died of his wounds a few days later."

Crompton paused looking like he was thinking back to that dreaded day. He gave a big sigh. His voice was barely above a whisper.

"Until you said his name I didn't know they had released him, never mind he was back in the city."

Crompton looked shaken as if a ghost had walked over his grave. He finished his drink, his hand tightly gripping the glass.

"Boss are you ok?" Monteith expressed his concern. "Yes, yes. Go home lads and get some rest. We will continue with this when you come back."

"You're sure?" Watson asked.

"Yes, go on. I've still got things to do."

As they left, Crompton deep in thought stood by the window looking down on the bright lights of the city centre.

Only one question was on his mind.

Why?

4

WEDNESDAY MORNING

MONTEITH AND WATSON had gone back home for a few hours' sleep around 2am.

They returned to the office for the 9.30am debrief following last night's shooting. Pathologist James Macintosh was there to present his initial findings and DCI Crompton holding court in his office. Strong coffee and bacon rolls from the cafe down the street, were the order of the morning, seeing as each of them had less than five hours sleep.

Crompton who had not been home, was still in his clothes from yesterday started the debrief.

"Ok folks let's get started. Mac, your findings, please."
"I've not done a full post mortem yet, but it's safe to say Ronald Freeman was shot at point blank range, through the head. In through the forehead and out through the back of the head. The two holes in the forehead suggest that the killer was outside the car and fired down

through the driver's side window. What's left of the bullets recovered from the car suggests they were 9mm. Forensics were still there completing their search of the car and the car park when I left around 2 a.m."

"Thanks Mac," Crompton said wiping his mouth with a

paper napkin after finishing his bacon roll and throwing it in the bin.

"We need to find out whether the shooter was in the pub with Freeman, waited until he left and shot him, or if the shooter was already waiting outside for him? Watson and Monteith can you go back and see if the landlord is up to answering any more questions, please. We need to know who visited the pub last night. Did anybody confront him whilst he was in there? Did he piss anyone off during the evening? I'll get uniform to carry out door-to-door enquiries in the area this morning."

Monteith put his coffee down on the desk.

"Boss, before we go, you said last night you knew Freeman and remembered why he got put away. Can you enlighten us?"

Crompton leaned back in his chair and gathered himself together, struggling with his thoughts.

"I had just become detective about two months earlier, and this was my first big case. Freeman entered Fred Mason's newsagents in the evening with a shotgun to rob it. He brandished the gun at the young girl behind the counter, Mason's daughter, and demanded the money from the till. Fred Mason was stacking shelves in the shop, and when he heard Freeman he came out and confronted him. Mason made a lunge for the gun to protect his daughter. During the struggle the gun went off. Mason suffered serious wounds to his chest and died in hospital two days later. Freeman ran out of the shop taking nothing. Up to that evening he had been only a petty criminal and been in prison before. Mason's daughter identified him from mug shots."

Crompton took a slurp of his coffee. "We were confident he would get put away for murder, but to our horror his lawyers were so good the jury only convicted him of manslaughter. He only got sixteen years in Craythorn Prison.

That was twelve years ago. That's why I was stunned he was out."

The room fell silent as they took in what he said. Monteith nudged Watson and caught Mac's eye. He signaled to the door to leave Crompton with his thoughts.

Monteith turned back and in a low voice said. "Boss, don't worry, we will catch the person who did this." Crompton looked up and nodded.

WATSON AND MONTEITH GOT BACK INTO THE BMW PARKED round the back of the headquarters and headed back to the Dragon's Den.

"Have you noticed that he is still shook up over this Freeman shooting?" Watson commented.

"I bet it's nothing. It's because as he said, Freeman was his first case." Monteith grinned.

"We all can remember our first cases when we joined. It was part of the thrill back then. Now they all seem to roll into one another. Ours was that drug bust at that cannabis factory. I remember still being high on the fumes the plants gave off the next day. The clearance team had to do it in twenty minute shifts because there were so many plants and they were affected by the fumes so much."

"Yes, I remember, but I don't know, I think there's something more to this," Watson sounded unsure.

"You're reading too much into it Terry, you should
lighten up." With that Monteith flattened the accelerator and shot down the high street.

"Slow down, slow down you, idiot. I don't want to end up on Mac's table just yet," Watson shouted grabbing onto the sides of his seat.

5

WHEN THEY GOT to the Dragon's Den, they found the press assembled behind the tape which had been strung up across the end of the road.

This would be a pain for the morning travellers as the pub was on a bus route. Once they were let through Monteith had to park his car on the road as crime scene tape was still across the gate leading to the car park. They showed their badges to the officer on the gate and ducked under the tape. As they walked around the side of the pub into the car park, forensics was packing away their gear into a white-paneled van.

"They look like beings from another planet when they're in all of their paper hazmat suits." Watson commented nudging Monteith.

"You've been watching too many sci-fi programs," Monteith joked back.

"I'm glad someone has something to laugh about," a woman shouted at them. She was standing by the pub's back door smoking. A small stout woman dressed in a knee-length black skirt, patterned blouse and thin cardigan.

"I'm sorry madam, it's just an internal joke. My name is Detective Monteith, and this is Detective Watson."

"I know who you are, I saw you last night. I'm Elizabeth Preston, follow me." She put her cigarette out on the wall and led them through the door, taking them into the main area of the pub.

The cleaners were going about their business as the three of them sat at a table in the lounge area.

"Is your husband around Mrs. Preston? We would like to ask him a few more questions about what happened last night," Watson asked

"I'm sorry, he is asleep in bed. After you left, the doctor came and gave him a sedative to calm him down and allow him to sleep. Any questions you have I can help you with," Elizabeth said resolutely.

"Where were you when Ronald Freeman was killed?"
"Murdered detective, don't you forget that," Elizabeth

spat back, detesting the two detectives in front of her. "I was upstairs. I'd put our two children to bed an hour before and stayed up there, until... you know what. I heard two loud bangs and went to look out of the window overlooking the car park. Peter, my husband, came running out from the back door. He went across to Ronald's car and looked through the window, then threw up by the wall. He then shouted up to call the police which I did."

"Did you see anybody else in the car park?"

"No," Elizabeth paused, "But I didn't think about it until now, I thought I saw the gate at the far end of the car pack swing shut before Peter came out."

"Where does that gate lead to?" Watson asked, jotting everything down.

"There is a large pathway which runs behind us and the other terrace houses on this side of the street. The refuse lorries and some delivery vans use it."

"Can you remember when you went upstairs who was down here Mrs. Preston?"

"Only Peter, Ronald and two other regulars who only live

across the street, so they would have gone out the front door. We'd a pool match earlier in the evening, but they'd all left by the time Peter had locked up."

A cleaner came into the lounge and started to polish the tables.

"Can you hang on June till we've finished?" Elizabeth asked her trying to keep calm.

"Oh, sorry," the cleaner said as she went back out. "Was Ronald a regular visitor?" Monteith continued with the questioning.

"Yes, three or four times a week he comes in." She paused. "Came in."

"Always the same days each week?" Watson asked. "Yes, when the pool or darts teams are playing at home. He didn't play, but he liked to cheer them on."

Watson and Monteith glanced at each other.

Mrs Preston noticed and sat up straight.

"Do you think someone planned this?" Her eyes were wide open with fright. Her mind going into overdrive with what the detectives were thinking.

"Well, we don't know yet, we have only just started the investigation. Did anyone cause him any trouble in here last night?" Watson tried to recover the situation.

"No," Mrs Preston said forcefully. "Now you should leave and get out and catch the bastard who killed him." With that she got up and turned away from them, standing staring through the front window, arms folded, and a look of despair on her face. Tears welling up.

Watson and Monteith got up and made their way to the door. Monteith stopped and said, "One last question Mrs. Preston. The address on his driver's licence is on the other side of town. Why did he make this pub his local?"

Elizabeth turned back to them with a confused look, "Don't you know? Ronald Freeman was my brother."

6

WEDNESDAY AFTERNOON

LITTLEWOOD WAS BACK on the move. He wanted to check on the next person on his list. Jackson Davis.

Of all the people he had marked down, this one made his skin crawl and his blood boil. Jackson had tortured and killed two prostitutes twenty-five years ago. Even though he had served his time and was in his early sixties, Littlewood was not prepared to let this murderer go unpunished. He had been watching Davis for about a week now, working out his routines.

Today, as always, he took his Alsatian for a walk in the park across the road from his house. Littlewood parked his red Skoda on a nearby street, locked it up and went into the park.

He wandered around for a couple of minutes taking in afternoon sun before sitting on one bench, not too close to Davis, but close enough to watch him. He picked up a newspaper, giving the impression he was reading in the afternoon sun, to anyone who passed by. The park was not one of the biggest in the city. It had big green spaces with pathways crisscrossing, flower beds were in full bloom, and trees lining the pathways around the edge. Mothers with small children making the most of the weather, getting out of the house with their kids for some fresh air.

Davis was there talking to the youngsters using the gym equipment teaching them the best way of doing dips and pull-ups on the bars. Davis may have been 62, but he still carried a big physical presence. Littlewood could visualise him trying to keep fit in the prison's gym, even though he thought prisons shouldn't have things like that.

Prison was a punishment and should not be a holiday camp, which he believed some had turned into. He had read in some on-line newspaper article that most prisons provided satellite TV and computer games for their guests at Her Majesty's Pleasure. One they said had a state of the art well-equipped gym. It angered him. More than £20 a month for Mr. Law-Abiding Joe Boggs on the outside, free for the scum on the inside. A complete waste of tax payer's money.

After about thirty minutes of watching and reviewing his surrounding Littlewood saw all he needed to. This takeout would be a lot harder than Freeman. A lot more planning was needed, and the park was not the place to do it. He would have loved to walk over to Davis and pulled the trigger on him there and then, but that was not how he wanted to do it. He wanted to savour Davis's demise, putting him through the same horrors the prostitutes suffered.

Returning to his car, he made notes in his red book, and left to plan Davis's demise.

JACKSON DAVIS HAD CLOCKED THE LONER ON THE BENCH.

A single man on his own, looking so far out of place in a park full of mothers and children, dog walkers, and teenagers doing teenage things. All he needed was a sign around his neck saying "loser."

He couldn't care less who he was, a father trying to get a

glimpse of his children after a divorce, the police doing undercover surveillance on somebody. Maybe him for all he knew. A looney fan trying to get close to him. They existed. There were other jailbirds he was in with who received so-called fan mail, from the public. Pen pals they called it. He couldn't work out who had fewer morals, the ones in jail or the ones that sent the letters.

Davis let the loner leave first, and then he said his goodbyes to the teenagers at the gym equipment. As he was going out of the gate, he put his dog's poo in the doggie bin. He crossed the road with his Alsatian by his side and up the gravel drive, passed his black Toyota RAV4 to his house.

He let his dog off the lead once they got into the house. The dog's tail wagged hard, his nose to the floor until he got to his water bowl for a long drink. Davis made his way up the carpeted stairs to his bedroom, opening the glass- fronted wardrobe and flicked through his stylish shirts. He smiled to himself as he picked out his outfit for this evening. Tonight he would go out on the town and have fun.

His kind of fun.

THEY WERE ALL GATHERED AROUND THE LARGE WHITE BOARD attached to the wall which held all the information they'd gathered on the case so far. It wasn't much other than the pictures of Ronald Freeman's body, slumped in the car. Gruesome that it was. Pictures of some things the forensics team found in the car park and pictures of what's left of the bullets. That was all.

"What else do we have?" Crompton said frustratingly.

He sat on the edge of one desk in the main office area. "The door to door came up with nothing. Nobody was around that time of night." Lorimer said, sitting at his desk looking at his notes. "One or two said they heard something but if they looked out of their windows, they saw nothing. The alleyway at the back of the houses is very dimly lit."

Crompton nodded and turned to Watson. "Did you get anything from Mr. Preston?"

"We didn't see Mr. Preston," Watson started. "But we spoke to his wife Elizabeth. She said she was Ronald's sister."

Watson watched his boss carefully in case there was any change in his face. Nothing.

"And?" Crompton pressed. He got off the desk and paced around waiting for answers.

"And she said Ronald came in three or four times a week. No problems with other customers. Nobody came in and caused him trouble. She may have seen the back gate open and close, but she cannot be certain. There could be hundreds of fingerprints on there."

"So, we have nothing from the crime scene, right?" A frustrated Crompton threw back at them. Everyone in the room went quiet and looked down so they could not catch the eye of the DCI.

Crompton stopped pacing and shouted,

"Right you lot, let's check on who his cellmates were in Craythorn. Are any of them out yet, has he kept in contact with anybody? Check his address out where is it?"

"His driver's licence gave an address in Thelwell." Monteith spoke up after Crompton's onslaught. "Right you two see what you find. Let's go to it." With that, Crompton stormed back to his office and slammed the door shut. The door shook, and the rest of the room exchanged glances.

Lorimer slowly shook his head. "Well that told us, is he always like that?"

"Only on his good days." Monteith laughed.

"Remind me not to be around on his bad days. I'll wear my riot gear if I am."

Watson and Monteith went back to their desks.

"What the hell are you playing at?" Monteith hissed. "I

saw you look straight at the boss when you said about Freeman's sister."

"There is something the boss is not telling us, I'm sure."

"You're nuts if you think that. You really believe he's holding something back?"

Monteith was pointing his finger in Watson's direction. "Yes, I do, but I don't know what yet."

Monteith grabbed his car keys off the desk and made for the door.

"Come on I don't want to spend a minute longer than I need to in Thelwell. Not in my car."

It's safe to say that Thelwell wasn't the best part of West Ravenswood. In fact, it was one of the worst areas. It was the biggest of the original council estates built when the city was redeveloped in the sixties. The Council put up the normal street sign "Welcome to Thelwell". One of the local ingenious Van Gogh's with his spray paint changed it to "Welcome to Thelwell HELL."

This was where most of the illegal activity in the city took place. You wanted drugs, you got them here, if you were looking for stolen property, the chances are you would find it here. Stolen cars were usually dumped here, either burnt out after the joy riders had finished with them, or if they weren't burnt out, they were being welded to another car to make a cut and shut.

The address the boys had for Freeman was a hostel on the edge of Thelwell. Monteith was glad it wasn't in the centre of hell, but still worried about his pride and joy as he pulled into the small car park at the front, which was surrounded by a low wall.

They slowly got out, looking around carefully, spotting the local look outs for the gangs in the area, kids, who had congregated on the street corner in front of a small newsagent.

"Let's make this quick. I don't want to come out and find I

have had my tyres slashed, or a key scraped down my paint work," Monteith said adamantly.

"Tenner to look after your car, mister." One kid shouted from across the road. "I'll do it for a fiver," another one chipped in then burst out laughing.

Monteith glanced back, over his shoulder as they went up to the front door. The hostel was a three-storey building dating back to when Thelwell was built. It started out as fancy flats but over the years, owners moved out and the squatters moved in. Now it had an electronic buzzer system you had to push before being allowed in. Watson pushed the button marked 'office.' There was a CCTV camera on the wall above the door. They waited about twenty seconds before a female voice answered.

"Yes, who is it?"

"Detectives Watson and Monteith, from the Criminal Detective Agency of the West Ravenswood Police Department madam."

"Show your IDs to the CCTV please."

They both took out their badges and held them up. The door buzzed and unlocked, and they stepped through into a large hall.

"Hello, I'm Sheila Evans, the manager here."

She was a tall thin lady, dressed in dungarees, yellow t-shirt and a bandana. They shook hands and Sheila directed them into her small office. She sat behind her desk, covered in paperwork and a computer. Watson looked around before sitting in one of the two guest chairs. The room was a tight squeeze, comprising the large desk, Sheila's chair, the two guest chairs, and two tall filing cabinets.

"What can I help you with detectives?" Sheila asked. "Ronald Freeman. His driver's licence gave this as his address?" Monteith started.

"Yes, he's been living here for about three months. It's very shocking his death." Sheila said with a quiver in her voice. "His sister rang this morning. Do you know who it was yet?"

"No, it's too early in the investigation to say anything. That's why we're here. What did you say, his sister Elizabeth rang this morning?"

"Yes, she is a regular visitor here, or should I say was. Visited Ronald about three times a week. Making sure he was ok for food and other things. He moved in here just after he came out of prison. His sister arranged the accommodation for him. Tried to get him back into mainstream life. She helped him to look for a job by going to the Job Centre with him and helped him to claim the benefits he was entitled to. She paid his rent as well. He spends, sorry spent, some evenings at her pub. Elizabeth mentioned about him moving into a flat nearer to where she lived."

Sheila started out of the window at the kids outside and then looked back at the detectives.

"You can't blame her for wanting him to live nearer to her. You know what this area is like."

"Did he have any other visitors besides his sister?" Monteith asked.

"No... not that I know of. But I heard him say a couple of times over the last week or so that he thought he was being followed. Elizabeth put it down to paranoia. Being cooped up in prison all that time watching your back and then released into society. I suppose you are bound to feel.... well vulnerable shall we say."

"Did he give you or his sister a description of the person he thought might be following him?"

"No, but you know what this area is like. Kids and other people hanging around the streets, looking after number one, or who pays them as look outs. He might have mistaken one of them. If there was a stranger around this area, then word soon gets out. The local grapevine stretches a long way and is quick."

"Any chance we can we look in his room?" Watson asked.

"I'm afraid I cannot allow that. Not unless you have a warrant and his sister is present. She has asked for nobody to go in for now." Sheila replied.

There was a knock on the office door. "Yes?" Sheila said.

A young man stuck his head round the door.

"Sorry didn't know you had company. Sheila, one of the bulbs has blown on the second floor landing."

"Ok Mike, I will be there soon thank you. Detectives, I'm sorry to cut this short but looks like I am wanted. No rest for the workers. I will see you out."

There were still kids and teenagers hanging around across the street by the shop. Monteith quickly went over to his car to check it still had four wheels, and the paint was intact.

"Do you get a lot of trouble with the kids round here?" Watson said to Sheila, as Monteith was franticly looking for his keys.

"Funnily enough no. They know what happens in this area stays in this area, and you do nothing to your neighbour. They look after their own here, including us. Hope you catch the bastard that did this."

With that Sheila disappeared inside.

7

MONTEITH DROPPED Watson back at his house.

It was a large four bedroom detached, in the South Meadows area of the city. It had taken them over an hour to get there from the hostel in Thelwell. A four car pile-up on the dual carriageway had added over an hour onto their usual 30 minute journey.

They were both tired and pissed off.

Watson walked up his gravel driveway past his blue Ford Focus and his wife Sally's red Citroen Xsara Picasso. The Picasso was on its last legs, but they needed to keep it going for now. He noticed the front lawn needed cutting, and the borders needed weeding and tidying up too. A job for the weekend he thought, already feeling exhausted at the prospect of gardening on his day off.

But what Watson needed right now was a hot shower, something to eat and hopefully, a massage from Sally.

He opened the front door to a wall of noise. How four people can make as much noise he would never work out, as he closed and locked the door behind him. Rachael was in her pink elephant pyjamas in the lounge, singing along loudly to her music.

The two oldest children, Simon 13 and 11-year-old Jason were arguing upstairs about something to do with a console game. Sally stood at the bottom of the stairs trying to regain order with her back to him. Watson took in her lovely figure, dressed in a tight red t-shirt, and a well- fitting pair of worn jeans. He smiled at the thought of that massage later and hoped Sally wouldn't be too tired.

The stairs doubled back on themselves. Coming off the hall was the lounge which ran the full length of the house, walls covered in photographs of family and signed framed posters of his favourite rock bands. The hall continued through to a large kitchen with all mod cons and red shiny cabinets. Off the kitchen was a toilet and wet room.

"Here's the cavalry," Sally said turning to smile at Terry.

"Nope, only The Lone Ranger, Tonto has just left." He pulled Sally into an embrace and kissed her gently on the lips.

"Daddy!" Rachael squealed as she spotted him and charged across the lounge and out into the hall. Terry bent down and picked her up, swinging her around, with her long hair flying behind her and her laughter filling the house.

"I'm listening to my music, here listen." With that she put her earphones on his head. Terry hadn't got the foggiest what he was listening to, but he bobbed his head along with it, trying to sing along with the words, making Rachael giggle and Sally shake her head in amusement. Rachael took the headphones back off his head.

"I was enjoying that," he said faking upset but with a big smile on his face.

"You're funny Daddy," Rachael said still giggling.

"Right young lady, I said you could stay up until Daddy came in," Sally broke the revelry.

"Aww he only just got in!" Rachael said with a pout. "Go on up angel. I'll come and say goodnight once you're ready for bed," said Terry herding her toward the stairs and clapping his hands, chuckling at her expression as she stomped upstairs.

"Food or shower first Mr. Lone Ranger," Sally said as she was wrapped up from behind in Terry's arms.

"Food first, I might need help in the shower later!"

"Oh, really?" Sally turned around with an impish grin on her face.

8

ON THE OTHER side of the city, Jackson Davis stopped his black Toyota RAV4 in Austin Lane, part of the red light district.

He wound down the passenger window and beckoned a small redhead over who was standing on her own next to a high wall. She was only 5ft 6ins in her red shiny high heels if that and wore a small shiny sequinned red crop top and a black leather look mini skirt which left nothing to the imagination.

"Fancy a good night?" she said through the window.

Davis smiled "Get in my dear, and I will give you the best night of your life."

But before she could open the door, Littlewood ran out of the dim light, shoved her out of the way, and piled into the back seat of Davis's car. He pulled out his Glock and pointed it at Davis.

"DRIVE NOW IF YOU KNOW WHAT'S GOOD FOR YOU," Littlewood bellowed.

Davis was stunned, wildly thinking about what he could do.

"DRIVE!" Littlewood shouted again, hitting the back of

the driver's seat to add emphasis to what he was saying.

Davis shoved his car in gear, and wheel spun it away from the curb.

"Drive where?" he said feeling the lump in his throat, and glancing in the rear-view mirror to try to glimpse this mad stranger who was in the back of his car by using the passing street lights.

"The Barton Industrial Estate. And if you see a police car or try to signal to anyone, I will shoot you right here and now." Littlewood said in calm and measured manner, settling back but still with his Glock trained onto Davis.

"What do you want? Money? My car? You can have it all. All you have to do is say, I'll pull over and you can take it."

Davis pleaded, still trying to work out who his unwanted passenger was. They moved out of the outer city centre on the main dual carriageway, and towards the Marsh Mills Trading Estate which Barton Industrial Estate was housed on.

Littlewood spoke with an authority in his voice. "Jackson Davis, former gym instructor. Jailed for torturing and killing two prostitutes twenty-five years ago. Released on licence. What would the authorities think if they knew you were bothering prostitutes again? Naughty, naughty."

"You have me at a disadvantage. You know all about me, but I don't know you."

Davis was confused, wondering who this mystery man was who knew all about him and his movements that night.

"Just shut up and drive."

As they came off the dual carriageway and entered the trading estate, they passed through a section of a well-lit road. Davis saw who his passenger was. A smile passed across his face, ending in a huge grin and a little laugh.

"What are you laughing at?" Littlewood said sitting forward a little with his hand gripping his gun a little tighter.

"Did you have a good time in the park today?"

"What are you on about?" Littlewood tried to remain

calm, but he felt a little flustered.

"Oh, come on Colin. That is your name isn't it? Colin Littlewood? You were in the park earlier on, watching me. You thought I hadn't noticed you?"

Davis was relaxing a little. Enjoying himself even. "Or should I say former Prison Officer Colin Littlewood? Medically retired through stress and a breakdown following the murder of your wife Jackie. I believe you were on the night shift at Craythorn Prison. Two kids broke into your house if I remember. Your wife disturbed them and… well…" Davis trailed off with a sly smile.

"How the fuck do you know that?" Littlewood had a sinking feeling that everything was unravelling in front of him.

"I was in Craythorn when it happened, surely you haven't forgotten that? It was all over the prison by the next day." Davis was trying to get himself on Littlewood's good side.

"Swing in through these gates on your right," Littlewood cut him short as they had arrived at the

Industrial Estate. Littlewood eased forward in his seat with his gun trained on Davis as he turned in. The Estate was a series of small boxy Industrial units four to a block. As they came through the gates, there were four units to their left and four others to their right, with parking bays for half a dozen cars in front of them. Each had roller doors as their main entrance for vehicles, and a small door which led to offices.

"Park over there."

Littlewood gestured with a wave of his gun to an industrial unit at the far end of one block. Davis parked up keeping his wits about him.

"When those two kids Thomas Smith and Andrew McNulty, were convicted, I heard they got a very warm reception from everybody at Black Lodge Young Offenders. Prisoners and screws alike. And again, when they were old enough to be transferred to Claythorn."

"Thank you for the update, but our little chat has run its course." With that Littlewood pulled the trigger and put a bullet into Davis's left thigh. Davis screamed in pain as blood flowed out of the wound, soaking his trousers.

"You tortured those prostitutes, so that's what I will do to you before... well... you know..."

"That's what you think." With that Davis put his foot hard down on the accelerator and aimed the car at the wall in front of them.

The car lurched forward and picked up speed. Littlewood was surprised, but got one more shot in at Davis which hit him in his left arm before he was thrown back in his seat. The car smashed into the wall at about thirty miles per hour. All the airbags went off leaving the inside of the car looking like a padded cell.

When Littlewood got his wits back, he looked around what was left of the car. Steam was rising from the front of the car; the radiator had split and hot water was spilling out. Bricks from the wall were all over what was left of the bonnet and some were inside because the windscreen had shattered and glass all over the place. Davis was already half out of the embedded car, trying to make a run for it. But with a bullet in his left arm and thigh, he was struggling.

Littlewood, still dazed from the crash, opened the back door and got out. Staggering around the back of the RAV 4, he saw Davis slumped in pain on the floor. He was clutching his thigh crying out in pain as the blood oozed out. Littlewood stood over Davis, and like a farmer putting an injured animal out of its misery he fired two more shots into Davis's chest.

"Two down," he said under his breath.

He stumbled back to the entrance of the Industrial Estate.

A car was parked with its engine running.

He got in.

9

Susan turned her little white Renault into the driveway at the front of the house.

She turned the engine off, got out and went round to open the passenger door. Putting an arm around her father's back and under his arm, she slowly helped him out of the car. He was groaning from pain with his injuries he'd suffered in the crash.

They'd worked together on the Jackson Davis take out. Susan had dropped off her father near to Austin Lane and pulled into a side street to make sure he was ok, and nothing went wrong. They knew Davis frequented prostitutes again through their tracking of him over the past few weeks. He'd tried to keep a low profile, using the ones new to the game, and so young they would not have been born when he'd killed before.

There were a few of the older ones milling around, still working the streets, who may have recognised him from before, but he stayed clear of the areas they usually worked.

Austin Lane was a relatively new place to find prostitutes. It used to be a good residential area, but it since had taken a dive when the big houses had been sold and made into flats of multiple occupancy. Unsavoury landlords and seedy people moved in and a new red light area came into force.

Her father knew which nights Davis liked to come here, and tonight was one of those nights. Susan sat in her car, avoiding the illumination from a nearby street light, with eyes on where her father was. She had the radio on down low listening to the local radio station and its late night music, humming away to the songs she liked, tapping in time on the steering wheel with her fingers.

After about twenty minutes she spotted Davis's car. It pulled up twenty yards away from where she was parked. A petite girl walked over to the car and leaned into the window. Then it all happened. She saw her father fly out from where he was standing, shoving the girl out of the way, and jumping into the back seat of Davis's car. A few seconds later the car took off down the road. Susan quickly started the engine and took off after them, nearly sideswiping another parked car as she pulled out. Her car's little engine raced as she tried to keep up with them. She followed them keeping a safe distance between them.

Susan and her father had worked out where they would take Davis to, The Barton Industrial Estate, but she was following just in case Davis had other ideas and cocked things up for them. After about fifteen minutes of travelling, she watched them turn into the industrial estate. She passed the gate and turned round, parking opposite the entrance. The road which led into the Industrial area was a no through road and deserted. Some nights lorries who had deliveries and arrived after the units has closed, parked up for the night. She'd a good view of where Davis had parked the car.

Susan gasped as without warning, Davis's car shot forward. The car smashed into the wall in front of them. Susan shouted out in horror as she witnessed what was happening. She was transfixed on the scene in front of her, unable to move, unable to help her father. Who'd survived the crash? Davis and not her father? Her father and not Davis? Were they both dead? Things had gone horribly wrong and she could do nothing about it.

After what seemed a long time, but in reality, was only a few seconds, she saw her father throw open the back door and fall out. He staggered around to the driver's side and two flashes lit up the floor, the car and the wall. Her father staggered through the gates and over to where she was parked. He got in, turned to her and whispered.

"Get me home."

Their next door neighbour was looking out of her bedroom window as they pulled into their driveway.

"Is he alright Susan?" she called out in a loud voice, as Susan helped her father out of the car.

"Yes, he's just had a few too many tonight," Susan replied, helping her father to the door while struggling to find her door keys in her pocket.

"Do you need any help? I can get my husband to come down."

"No Mrs. Banks thanks, I can manage."

With that Susan got the front door open and eased her father into the house. She stood him up against the wall and locked the door.

"What did that fucking bitch want?"

"Dad, that's enough" Susan said firmly.

She guided him down the hall past the lounge and into the kitchen at the back of the house. Slowly she eased his arms out of his coat and sat him down at the table.

"AARRGH my neck," Littlewood cried out. He was suffering badly from the crash.

"My arm is killing me."

"You have whiplash from the crash and you must have

bashed your arm against the door when you hit the wall." Susan was getting a bowl of hot water ready and retrieving the medical box from the back of a kitchen cupboard.

"What the hell happened?"

"The bastard recognised me," he said through gritted teeth. Half through the pain he was in, half through annoyance and frustration. He slammed his hand on his good right arm onto the table. The few items which were already on the table jumped with the ferocity.

"What? How?" Susan stood in the middle of the kitchen staring at her father in bewilderment.

Littlewood spent the next half an hour telling her every detail of the conversation he had with Jackson Davis, in-between the shouts of pain and curses as Susan tended to his wounds and strains.

When she'd finished with dressing his wounds and dosing him up with pain killers it was almost 1am. Susan guided her still shaken father through the hall and up the stairs to his bedroom, picking up his coat on the way up. She helped to undress him and made sure he was comfortable in bed, then sat on the edge of it.

"I want you to lie low for a few days, please Dad. You need to gain your strength and recover from this." Susan reproached. He knew it was no good arguing with her.

"You've almost risked everything in taking down Jackson Davis, including your life. And I don't like it. It was stupid and careless. The police will be all over this from now on, and we need to be careful in what we do and how we do it."

"You're right" Littlewood said wincing in pain. The painkillers had not taken effect yet.

"I know I'm right," Susan replied. "Good night Dad." Susan kissed her father on his forehead and got up.

She went over to his coat on a nearby chair removing his gun from the pocket and stared at it. She then opened his wardrobe and took out the rucksack putting the gun in it and took out the red book. Opening it she put a line through the name of Jackson Davis. She looked at the other names her father had on the list.

Smiling to herself as she returned the book to the rucksack and it to the wardrobe.

10

THURSDAY MORNING

WATSON AND MONTEITH arrived at the Barton Industrial Estate after being diverted there from their way in to the station.

They showed their IDs to the constable assigned to guard the gate. He pointed them toward the crashed car. Just inside the gate, a group of about a hundred members of the public were gathered behind a section of crime tape. Workers from some of the industrial units, who had turned up for a normal day's work, only to find today would not be a normal day.

"Ladies and Gentleman, Boys and Girls," Monteith burst out as they went past them. "Here they are the finest detectives in the city, Keith Monteith and Terry Watson, hhhuurrraayyy." Monteith added a mock wave.

Watson tried not to laugh but failed miserably.

Monteith parked up, and they surveyed the scene as they got out. What was left of the Toyota RAV4 was imbedded in the wall of one of the units. The rear left passenger door was open as was the driver's door. By the driver's door a white tent covering a body. Mac was busy buzzing around the tent. Two forensics chaps were taking pictures of the inside of the car. Next to the closest industrial unit to the crash, the police were taking statements from two people, who looked like they worked there.

"Morning boys. What a lovely day."

Mac got up from what he was doing and met them as they were approaching the car.

"I swear you love your job too much," Monteith joked. "Why are we here? Is it not just an abandoned crashed car?"

"Body under the tent has four bullet holes in him. My guess 9mm. Will find out when I get him back to the morgue."

Mac took them over to the body and after they had put on protective shoe coverings and gloves, he held back the tent opening for them to enter. Jackson Davis was on his back. His eyes were open full of horror. His chest was dark red with the blood from the two bullet holes. Blood had also pooled under his left side from the wounds in his leg and arm.

"Thanks Mac, we've seen enough," Watson said as he followed the trail of blood which led from where Davis lay under the tent and to the driver's door.

He looked in through the door. Blood was all over the front seats and down by the gear stick. He couldn't see much due to the airbags deploying in the car, the broken windscreen, the bricks, and the crumpled dashboard. Monteith joined him. "Certainly, no accident, but what happened first? The shots in the leg and arm, or the crash?" Watson mused. "The chest shots were definitely fired outside the car.

There's not enough room in the back of the car to do them."

"Hopefully one of these units has working CCTV that will show something," Monteith pondered. "I'll get one of the PC's to ask around."

He turned to Mac, "See you later in the morgue for your update."

Mac waved in their general direction as he continued to gather evidence.

"Detectives?" One of the PCs who was getting statements called across to them. Watson and Monteith turned and walked across to see what he had found.

"This is Mr. Holland. He found the car and body."

Mr. Holland was dressed in blue work overalls and steel toe capped boots. His unit housed a small engineering business.

"I arrived about 7.30am as normal. I saw the crashed car as I came through the gates. I first thought it was left there by a joy rider. We get a few cars left here, some smashed up, and some burned out. It was not until I got closer I saw the body. I rang the police as soon as I unlocked my unit."

"Did you go near the car or touch anything before the police arrived?" Watson said.

"No," Mr. Holland said emphatically. "Me and a couple of others went round as people arrived telling them to keep back, not only because of the body, but also because the unit could be unsafe."

Watson nodded. "Did you see anyone else in the area, hanging around either on foot or in a car you did not recognise?"

Mr. Holland shook his head. "No. Only the regular cars owned by the workers here who come in around the same time as me."

Before Watson had a chance to ask any more questions, there was a commotion over where the public were being kept back. Bursting through was a man in a suit and tie. He was walking purposely over to the crime scene. Two of the PCs were trying and failing to stop him.

"What the fuck is happening? Why we are being stopped from entering the estate and working," he shouted as he made his way across the tarmac.

"Excuse me, sir," Watson held his hand out in a stop signal as he met the man coming towards them. "Who are you?"

"It does not matter who I am, why are we being stopped?"

"I heard you the first time, as did everyone around here," Watson cut him off mid-sentence and was trying to keep his cool. "Again, I would like to know who you are?"

"The name is McGill, James McGill if you really need to know. I own some of the businesses on here, and you are stopping me from getting out my deliveries. Time is money don't you know."

He was a large chap, in stature. Watson had seen it all before. Men acting with bravado because of their size. The bigger they are, the harder they fall he reminded himself before responding.

"Well, excuse me Mr. McGill. We have a crime scene here and until we have finished, I'm afraid that this estate will remain closed. Please, can you return to behind the tape?" Watson talked with a measured calmness in his voice.

"What! For a crashed car which some little joy riding prick crashed. Haven't you got better things to do?" McGill was indignant with rage at being told what to do by someone, who in his opinion was below him.

With that Watson lost his cool, in a big way.

"Let me fucking show you if you want to," he bellowed in McGill's face.

With that he grabbed McGill by the scruff of the collar and dragged him around the car to where Jackson Davis's body was.

"Hey what are you doing? Get the fuck off me," McGill stammered, trying to keep his feet. Watson flung back the flaps of the tent and shoved McGill in, following right behind.

"Does this look like a joy riding prick to you? Well?"

Mac and another man were sealing up the body bag to transport Davis's body back to the morgue. McGill could only see the top half of Davis's body, but it was enough for him.

He gasped at the sight in front of him. He gulped, ran out of the tent and threw up on the floor. After he had tidied himself up, Watson was waiting for him. Standing face to face he lowered his voice.

"Piss off back to your businesses, or I will arrest you for obstruction of a police crime scene. Do you understand?" McGill nodded nervously. Still feeling nauseous he wandered off muttering under his breath. Mac appeared at Watson's shoulder watching McGill trying to regain his composure in front of everyone who was standing nearby.

"Interesting policing," he commented glancing down at the pile of sick that McGill had left. "Good job forensics has finished or they would curse you for contaminating the area".

Back in the car, Monteith had a smirk on his face. They were driving back to the station, following the private ambulance which carried the body of Davis back to Mac's morgue for a more thorough investigation.

"What?" Watson glanced at Monteith.

"I was wondering, when did they teach us what you just did at the police academy because I can't have been in the class that day. Either I was ill or in bed with that blond called Carol."

"Oh, piss off!" Watson replied. They both burst out laughing. When it died down Watson queried, "You and Carol?"

Monteith smirked again. "Just a little homework with handcuffs."

They both burst out laughing again.

Their laughing stopped, and the smiles were wiped off their faces when they entered their office in the station.

11

"MONTEITH, WATSON GET IN HERE!"

Crompton bellowed to them from his office doorway as soon as he saw them. He was not alone. Superintendent Grant Matthews was waiting for them too.

Lorimer leaned back in his chair and smiled as they went past.

"Do you want to borrow my riot gear?" Watson smiled back and gave him the finger.

When they got to his office, Crompton was sitting behind his desk looking very pissed off, and the superintendent was standing ramrod straight looking out of the window. Matthews' uniform immaculate with creases so sharp they could cut glass. His black hair looked like it had been painted on, with not one hair out of place. His shoes shone so much they gleamed.

Watson and Monteith didn't even get into Crompton's office before the superintendent turned and started his rant. "What the hell did you think you were doing?"

"Pardon?" Watson looked blank as he came through the door.

Everyone outside stopped what they were doing and listened in on the argument which was brewing.

"You know exactly what I am on about. That stunt you pulled at the industrial estate. I have had a very irate and angry James McGill on the phone. He said you assaulted him," Matthews continued.

"The jerk was interfering in the crime scene. He would not get out of the way, and he was acting as if he owned the place," Watson tried to explain.

Matthews was in no mood for explanations and he continued his rant pointing his finger at Watson.

"That was no excuse to do what you did. I had to calm him down, because he was going to press charges against you, but I talked him out of it. You are lucky he is not taking this further."

"I'm lucky? He's lucky that he's not sitting in a jail cell."

"Enough. Kenneth, either you get your detectives in order or they will be back on beat duty before they know it."

With that Superintendent Matthews grabbed his hat off the desk and threw open the door. He marched out into the outer office, his face like thunder. Everyone out there averted their gaze and busied themselves to avoid eye contact.

Before they could ask about what just happened, Crompton put his hand up, got up from his desk and closed the door.

"How the hell did Matthews get involved?" asked a stunned Monteith.

Crompton sat back at his desk.

"Because it's not what you know, but who you know. McGill and Matthews know each other from the golf club."

"But McGill behaved like a dickhead, Terry's right, we could have arrested him."

"And he would have been out before you completed your paperwork. McGill may be a dickhead, but he is a dickhead with connections, and connections which control all of us."

Crompton sighed. "But… I must admit I wish I had been there to see what you did." Crompton's face lit up with a big grin and the laughter returned.

"OK, so what do we know about what happened with this crashed car and the body?" Crompton asked as they moved back into the main office. Lorimer brought them up to speed.

"Just to backtrack on Freeman, the door-to-door visits came up with nothing. And when we tracked his cell mates, most were still in prison and those who had been released had left the area. As for last night, according to the DVLA, the car belongs to a Jackson Davis; address Manor Street, recently released from Craythorn Prison."

"Another ex-prisoner, two in two days, coincidence?" Monteith put the question out to everyone. Nobody said anything, pondering what he said.

"What was he in for?" Crompton asked. Lorimer continued his round up.

"He was jailed for the torture and killing of two prostitutes twenty-five years ago. Released on licence six months ago."

"OK?" said Monteith leaning back in his chair "We have two ex-prisoners both jailed for killing people, both shot dead months after coming out, strange coincidence? Or do we have a weird serial killer?"

The others looked at each other contemplating the huge impact on the city if it was a serial killer.

"Apart from the fact they were both in jail, it seems a bit of a tentative link. How many get released each year from prison, thousands? And because two get shot in two days there's a nutter running loose. What do we do, stop them releasing prisoners?" Watson said dismissively.

"No, but I think it's something we should think about." "Somebody must have held a grudge for a long time in that case, which is doubtful. Freeman was in for what… twelve years, Davis for twenty-five. No, I don't buy it."

Crompton cut in.

"Right Lorimer, you take two other officers and go to Davis's address. See if he has any family and talk to the neighbours. Keith, Terry both of you go and see if Mac has started on Davis's autopsy."

THE MORTUARY WAS BASED AT THE CITY'S HOSPITAL, IN THE Bereavement Care Centre.

Monteith parked in the private bays around the back of the hospital. Entering through a set of double doors and down into clinical clean anteroom.

Both heard the blasting music coming from Mac's morgue before they even entered it. They opened the frosted glass door to the sound of AC/DC's classic Highway to Hell.

Mac was sitting at his desk going through some files, singing at the top of his voice.

He looked up to see the pair of them head banging and playing air guitar.

"You two look like right pillocks!" He said bursting out laughing as he turned the music off.

"That's loud enough to wake the dead!" Monteith came back with, shaking his head trying to regain his hearing.

"We have great sing along's down here me and my mates," Mac said going over to the freezer drawers. He opened one. "Jane Doe here has got a wicked voice."

"You're nuts Mac. So, what are these two, backing singers?"

Watson was pointing to the two covered bodies on the tables.

"No. These are fresh in today. Couple killed in a head on collision with a lorry. Driver fell asleep at the wheel. They didn't stand a chance. I was just going over the paperwork before examining them. Want to stay and watch?" Mac picked up a scalpel and a hacksaw from the table of instruments, looking at them longingly as if they were his pride and joys, which they were.

"No fear. You couldn't even pay me to watch you do what you do in here. It's bad enough to look at the bodies at a crime scene," Monteith said adamantly as he backed away to the door.

Watson said, "Ok Mac, before Keith faints or does something else, we came down to see if you had anything on Jackson Davis. Have you examined him yet?"

"Nope. He has been prepped by my colleague and is through in the other room. As you can gather, we are rather busy at the moment. Would you gentleman like to come through here and I can introduce you to the late Mr. Davis?"

Mac opened the swinging doors to the adjacent room and held them open for them to follow.

"I think I will wait here Mac, I can see perfectly well from here." Monteith said as he came through the door and spotted the covered body on the aluminium table.

"Feeling squeamish, are we?" Mac tried to goad him. "No! I will… well stay here."

"Ok Terry you all right with this?"

"Yep let's see him."

With that Mac pulled the sheet off Davis's naked body. "Right we have four bullet wounds. Looking at the ones on the upper leg, here, and the arm above the elbow, here, the angle of the wounds suggests that the killer was sitting behind him on the backseat. The two in the chest were done outside of the car.

Judging by the angle of them, the killer was standing above him and firing down.

The broken ribs, cuts and bruises to the chest, legs and head came from the crash."

"Are the bullets still in him?" Terry asked.

"No. I've already taken them out and given them to

ballistics," Mac said as he turned and picked up another scalpel. "Sure, you won't stay?"

They both spun around hearing the doors fly open, and Monteith flying out through them.

"I think I'll pass. Looks like I've a detective to catch."

———

SERGEANT LORIMER, WITH TWO FEMALE CONSTABLES ARRIVED IN a squad car at Davis's house in Manor Street, taking in what the surrounding area was like.

The park across the road was busy, and the traffic on the road was light. They walked up the drive towards the house. The curtains were drawn both upstairs and downstairs. As they approached, there was movement behind the curtains downstairs as the head of an Alsatian poked through. It barked nonstop when it saw them.

"Oh, what a lovely dog," one of the constables said.

Lorimer looked at her. "You say that now when it's safe in the house. Let's see what you think when we get in there."

With that he knocked hard on the front door. The Alsatian flew at the door banging it hard barking loudly, defending its territory.

"Is it still a lovely dog now?" Lorimer turned and smiled at the constable.

"Hello? Excuse me?" An old gentleman was walking up the driveway, waving. He was dressed in a shirt and cardigan with smart trousers and dark shoes.

Lorimer turned and walked towards him. "Can I help you?"

"I'm sorry; my name is Donald Carter. I saw your car from my house next door. Are you after Jackson Davis?"

He was curious to find out why they were there.

"Do you know Mr. Davis well sir?" Lorimer asked. "Not personally. I spoke more to his parents. Very nice couple.

Jackson keeps himself to himself. Very weird man. When he was jailed for those murders his parents never got over it. It was a big shock for them."

"When did you last see Mr. Davis?" Lorimer pulled out his notebook.

"Let me see. I remember last night seeing his car here about 9.30pm. But when I looked out around 10pm before I went to bed, it wasn't here."

"Ok, thank you for that." Lorimer jotted it down. "There is no answer from the house. Have you seen his parents? We need to talk to them."

"You will have a job doing that. His father died about four years ago. Cancer, very quick. His mother is in a home. Jackson had to put her there about three months ago for her own safety. Alzheimer's, poor woman doesn't know what day it is half the time. The wife and I looked after her after his father died, and before he came out."

Lorimer was noting it down, having trouble keeping up.

He turned to one of the constables. "We will need a locksmith and a dog warden." She nodded and disappeared towards the squad car to make the arrangements.

"Why are you doing that? I'm sure Mr. Davis will be back later."

The neighbour was looking worried.

"I'm sorry to say, but Mr. Davis was involved in an accident last night and has died." Lorimer informed the neighbour.

"Oh god, oh no. How terrible!" the neighbour exclaimed. He paled immediately and looked very shocked.

Lorimer beckoned the other constable over. "Can you take him back to his house, and stay with him until he is ok please?"

She led the neighbour away leaving Lorimer with his thoughts.

He had never been involved with a major murder enquiry

before. Prior to this secondment he was in charge of the outlying police stations dealing with delegating work, supervising investigations, monitoring law enforcement operations, supervising responses to critical incidents and managing resources.

Now building up to his Detective Sergeants exam this was his big chance to impress, and he was looking forward to doing just that.

12

SATURDAY

A COUPLE of days had passed before Littlewood felt he was well enough to venture out.

Maybe a visit to his wife's graveside. But it was to be done with the strict ruling from Susan that he was only to go there and back, and not to try to do anything else. She was worried that he would start looking for another person on his list, and he wasn't mentally nor physically fit enough for that yet.

He called into the florists first for some flowers to put on the grave. Red roses, Jackie's favourites. They had grown them in both the front and back garden at their house. Jackie was always found outside, tending to them, dead heading, spraying, and keeping the weeds down.

Littlewood smiled sadly at the memory of his late wife.

Parking his Skoda in the small car park outside the local council cemetery and collecting the roses off the back seat, he entered through the large gates. The sun was shining bright and as it came through the leaves on the trees, it left a dappled look on the paths. There were a couple of other people visiting their deceased loved ones, both in their own world. A fresh grave was being dug in a far corner of the already overcrowded cemetery. Reaching Jackie's granite headstone, he knelt and placed the roses against it. Tracing his hand over the inscription again as he always did.

Her Life A Beautiful Memory, Her Absence A Silent Grief.

After a silent prayer, he got up and sat on a nearby bench to gather his thoughts. His mind drifted back to when he first saw Jackie, at the local sixth form college. They had attended different secondary schools prior to sixth form, Colin leaving with 10 O Levels, and Jackie Farmer with 8. Soon they became inseparable, spending as much time together as they could. He remembered their first holidays together. None parent holidays. Nothing extravagant like jetting off to Ibiza or the Canary Islands, more B&B holidays on the sun-drenched coast of Britain walking along cliff paths. Exploring off the beaten track villages and secluded beaches.

University for both of them was never on the cards, so they worked for local firms saving money for a deposit on their first flat. They were married soon after Jackie's 20th birthday, and eleven months later Susan arrived.

Colin started working at Claythorn Prison as a prison officer, and they moved into the house they were to call home for the next ten years. It should have been the whole of their life, well into retirement but twelve years of marriage to his childhood sweetheart was ended in one night, ten years ago.

A wife, a mother, and a friend, taken from him and his daughter.

There could have been two people in that grave if they had not allowed Susan, who was ten years old back then, to stop around a friend's house for a sleep over. He had been on a night shift at Craythorn Prison.

On his way into work he dropped a very excitable Susan at her friends. The shift was as uneventful as it could be until his boss called him in to the wing office. An hour later he was at his wife's bedside in the hospital's emergency ward crying, almost inconsolable. She was on a life support system with severe head injuries, a broken arm and two broken ribs.

He was told by the police that his next door neighbour Mr. Banks, who was giving his dog a late night walk, saw two teenagers running out of the back gate of his house. They had nearly knocked him over in their effort to get away. Mr Banks went inside through the open back door, and he found Jackie at the bottom of the stairs not moving. Blood was pouring from the head injuries she had suffered. He called 999 straight away.

The police and an ambulance arrived soon after, rushing Jackie to hospital and securing the house. Judging by the mess the house was in, the two teenagers were in the process of ransacking it when his wife had disturbed them. She had either been pushed or fallen down the stairs.

With the description Mr. Banks gave, and the fingerprints left at the scene, Thomas Smith and Andrew McNulty were arrested three days later. Charged with burglary and initially, GBH with intent. This was upgraded to murder when Jackie died of her injuries a week later without regaining consciousness.

At the trial. both Smith and McNulty pleaded guilty to burglary but not guilty to murder. The jury found them also not guilty of murder, but guilty of manslaughter. They didn't reach a murder charge because they couldn't decide if Jackie had slipped and fallen down the stairs or was pushed by one of Smith or McNulty. They received ten years.

In the intervening years, Littlewood found himself in a very dark place. Depression set in. The Black Dog it was called by some people who suffered from it. Drink also became a good friend.

He tried to go back to work following months off with his depression. When he was at work he either smelt of booze or arrived drunk. The end came when he was disciplined for hitting a prisoner who goaded him over his wife's death. He was medically discharged from the prison service soon after.

It was then he started to formulate a plan to get his own back.

13

MONDAY

LITTLEWOOD PARKED up at the end of a long tree lined lane.

Along one side were fourteen poplar trees, stretching so high it almost looked like they were touching the sky. Behind them, fields planted with various crops.

On the other side of the lane, were large fancy houses and country retreats. They were big enough to hold a party in and not disturb the neighbours. They were an estate agent's gold mine. If your company bagged selling one on the odd occasion that one came up for sale, you're quids in on commission.

The lane was on the edge of a little village, five miles to the North of West Ravenswood. It was picture postcard view in the spring and summer, but a pain to get out of in the winter snowfalls.

Littlewood was looking at the house at the very end of the lane. Number 10, also called Horizons. He had been here before with his wife Jackie. But that was in better times. They used to be invited by the owner and his wife to the numerous parties they held there. Team building, he used to call it. Drunken revelries would be a better description of the night's events.

Littlewood alighted from his car and walked the few metres to the entrance of the driveway. Two brick pillars with large granite balls on top, leading to a brick laid driveway which was large enough for five or six cars. Only one was parked there now, a brand new Mercedes C-Class. Well-kept holly hedges bordered the front garden. The house had a stunning mock Tudor style frontage.

He knocked on the front door twice, but no answer came. Littlewood walked away down the side of the house, with the detached double garage to his left. He could hear a lawn mower as he opened the side gate which led to the vast back garden. A swimming pool was in front of the patio doors. Beyond that was a huge lawn surrounded by large shrubs and trees. Riding on a sit on lawn mower was the owner of this grand house, the person Littlewood came to see.

Retired prison governor Adrian Knowles reached the far end of the lawn, turned the lawnmower around and headed back towards the house. He looked up and noticed somebody standing on his patio. Littlewood waved as he saw Knowles coming towards the house. Knowles parked up by the patio and turned the lawnmower off.

"Can I help you? How did you get in here?" Knowles was puzzled as he walked towards the intruder.

"It's me, sir. Colin, Colin Littlewood."

"Colin? Oh yes I remember, from Claythorn."

Knowles seemed to remember but was still unsure. "How long has it been?" He held out his hand for Littlewood to shake.

"Eight years since Claythorn. Ten years since Jackie." Littlewood's voice still cracked a bit, when talking about his late wife.

"That long! I didn't realise it was that long ago. Since I retired from the service one day rolls into another. How is your daughter? Susan isn't it?"

"She has coped ok, better than me in some ways. She had

her bad days and weeks, but now she works as an administration manager at a local firm."

"And you? How are you doing?"

Knowles had visibly relaxed and felt at ease with his visitor. Littlewood's little history cameo was working.

"That's why I came to see you, Sir. I need help in getting back into the job market. I have had a couple of short-lived jobs since the service but I was hoping you could help. But I can see you are busy. I was wrong to just turn up, I'm sorry," Littlewood said as humbly as he could. He turned as if to walk away.

Knowles put a hand on Littlewood's shoulder.

"No… no don't go. Please come inside and we will talk and see what we can come up with. After what you went through, it's the least I can do."

He led the way through the patio doors into the large living room. Two three seater wine coloured sofas dominated the room. They faced each other with a glass topped wooden table between them. A landscape picture hung over an open fire. A 60 inch plasma TV hung on the opposite wall, with surround sound speakers. At the far end of the room, a six seated dining room table.

They went on into the kitchen. For such a big house it was surprisingly small. Knowles picked up the kettle.

"Tea or coffee?"

"Neither," Littlewood replied.

Knowles swung round to find Littlewood standing in the doorway with a gun pointing to him.

"Colin? What is this?"

"Sit down now!" Littlewood shouted.

Knowles put the kettle down and slowly sat down on one of the wooden chairs at the table. Not taking his eyes off the gun.

"Colin, whatever it's I'm sure we can work something out."

"Too late for that. I needed help ten years ago but got nothing. My wife was murdered, and I got no help"

Littlewood approached the table with hate in his eyes.

This was more personal than Freeman and Davis.

"No help? We gave you a lot of help. As much time off as you needed. Close to six months wasn't it. We arranged bereavement counselling."

"COUNSELLING!! Is that what you called it? It was crap, no help at all. The counsellor needed more help than I did."

"We put you on shifts to help you look after Susan. Not putting you back on the wings so you could settle back into work. If I remember, you were in the prisoner reception area when you came back. You only had to work days and no weekends. We were all happy for you and Susan when McNulty and Smith got what they deserved." Knowles tried to take the tension out of the situation.

"They murdered Jackie. They should have got more, but that sodding jury were conned by the so-called evidence."

Littlewood screamed back in Knowles's face. He then lost it and hit Knowles over the head with the gun twice. Blood started to poor down his face.

Knowles rubbed the blood away from his eyes and nose as he tried to speak.

"But then you ruined your career by turning up for work drunk or missing your shifts altogether. And putting Freeman in the hospital with a broken nose was the final straw. I couldn't protect you after that."

Littlewood's mind disappeared back to that fateful day. One of the few days he was sober enough to go to work. The prisoner reception area was where the newcomers to the prison had to relinquish their possessions and outside clothing before being given their prison clothes. Officers oversaw this but serving prisoners could work in there as a privilege. One of those was Ronald Freeman.

Littlewood although sober was in a foul mood and giving

grief to anyone around him. There had been six newcomers that day. As Freeman was giving out clothes to one newcomer, Littlewood shouted at him to hurry it up and pushed him out of the way. Freeman gave back a verbal volley about the death of Littlewood's wife. Littlewood replied with two swift punches to the face before being restrained by other officers.

Freeman landed in hospital with a busted nose, and Littlewood ended up being sacked for gross misconduct. Knowles sensing that Littlewood was not paying full attention went to get out of his chair.

"Colin, please. Let's try to work something out. I can help you get the help you need."

"I don't need help from you." Littlewood fired two shots into Knowles chest. Knowles staggered backwards and fell up against the kitchen side, sliding down onto the floor. Blood pooled around his body quickly.

Putting the gun into his jacket pocket, Littlewood turned and walked out of the kitchen back into the living room. He looked out of the patio windows, making sure he was not seen by the neighbours.

Quickly he made his way back to his car. Opening the

door, he slumped into the seat. Emotion that had built up during the argument with Knowles rushed out of him and he burst into floods of tears. It took a lot out of him, thinking about his wife, and killing Knowles, who was once a colleague, a friend.

Susan arrived at her place of work at 8.45am, parking her white Renault in the employees' car park.

The morning sun was so bright, she kept her sunglasses on while walking towards the front door. Staff were talking between themselves of what they did during the weekend and muttering about the workday ahead.

The main reception area was made purposely unwelcoming. All the floors and walls were grey tiled. The reception desk was behind security glass and always manned by two people. CCTV cameras had been placed both inside and outside of the main door. No personal effects could be taken through into work areas. Employees' had to put their belongings into lockers before entering.

Susan showed her ID to the reception staff and was buzzed through the sets of doors leading to her office. She walked along the carpeted corridor, called into the mail room, and picked up a pile of files. In her office she put the files down on her desk and searched through them for two in particular. Once found, she opened her handbag and brought out two pieces of photocopied paper.

She inserted one in each file and then put the files back in with the others.

14

TRYING to get three kids out of bed, washed, dressed and fed was akin to military action in the Watson home.

Simon and Jason were first as they always left before the others. Simon was in year 7 at South Meadows Academy. Jason was in the last year at the local primary. As both schools were next to each other, they walked together. Sally, a teacher at the primary school, took Rachael in with her.

Watson was polishing off toast and coffee while watching BBC Breakfast News. His phone went off breaking the tedium of wars, politics and so called celebrities at glitzy parties. It was Monteith, and he was not happy.

"Can you pick me up today? I have car problems."

"Yes sure. What's up with your pride and joy?"

"You will see when you get here." With that Monteith had gone.

Watson looked at his phone confused. He turned the television off and took his mug and plate into the kitchen.

"Who was on the phone?" Sally asked. She was getting Rachael ready by the front door, putting her coat on.

"Keith. He wants me to drive today. Says he has car problems but wouldn't say what."

"He's probably only got it dirty and didn't want to be seen out in it. I swear he spends more time with that car than with Katie and the kids," Sally said with disdain. "We're off now. Come on Rachael."

Rachael ran and wrapped her arms around her dad's legs, then skipped out through the front door with her bag strapped to her back.

"He's not that bad. I would be careful if I had a car like his."

"There's careful and then there's neurotic. And he borders on being neurotic over that car." Sally said back. With that she was out of the door.

Watson pulled into the street where Monteith lived. His car was being loaded onto the back of a recovery vehicle. Monteith and his wife Katie were having a full blow argument in the front garden. Their children, 10- year-old Rebecca and 5-year-old Pixie were looking out of the lounge window.

Watson jumped out of his car and raced over. He looked at the car being loaded and noticed that it had had all its tyres slashed.

"What the hell happened?"

"Ask him!" Katie bellowed. "He's fucked everything up."

With that she stormed into the house slamming the front door behind her.

"What does she mean?" Watson asked in bewilderment.

"It's nothing," Monteith was dismissive.

"Nothing? Katie's running around screaming at you.

Your car has its tyres slashed, and you're saying it's nothing. What the hell has happened?"

"Let's get out of here. I need breakfast."

Twenty minutes later Monteith was tucking into a full English breakfast. They had driven in silence to the cafe near to their headquarters.

"So are you going to tell me what happened back there?"

Watson kept his voice low. The cafe was packed with customers. Some of the night-shift beat coppers were in their winding down.

"The car is a warning," Monteith said between mouthfuls.

"A warning? From who?" Watson was confused.

"Jimmy Russell."

"Russell?! What have you done to anger that lunatic?" Watson tried to keep his anger in check and his voice low as a waitress came by the table. "Russell is not one to get on the wrong side of. You should know that."

Monteith slurped his tea and then stared down into the cup, avoiding Terry's eyes.

"I owe him money. Gambling debts."

"How much do you owe?" Terry asked warily, not really wanting to know the answer.

"Nothing much, just five grand," Monteith replied as if it was nothing.

"You owe Jimmy Russell five grand?!" Watson was losing his temper. "You fucking idiot."

Watson got up and stormed out of the cafe. Monteith just looked at him in stunned silence. His fork halfway to his mouth. Other customers were looking over. Monteith put his fork down and wiped his mouth composing himself. "Have you not seen a domestic before?" he called out to the cafe residents and then walked out of door.

Watson was sitting in the car, with the engine running. His face still contorted with anger. Monteith slowly got into the passenger seat.

"You need to get yourself sorted out," Watson said staring straight ahead out of the windscreen. "You almost fucked up your marriage before it began with your gambling. And judging by Katie this morning, you are well on the way to doing it again."

"She'll be fine." Monteith acted as if nothing was wrong.

"FINE… FINE… It's a wonder she's not ripped your balls off. Listen to yourself. You have a family to look after now."

Watson pulled out into the traffic and headed for their headquarters.

"We are already looking for one psychopath for these murders. I don't want to go looking for another one in Russell because something has happened to you."

15

THE OFFICE WAS DECIPHERING what the newspapers, both local and national, were saying about the shootings.

Putting two and two together and making five. Sensationalism as only newspapers can pull off, even though they had the official statement put out by the Police Press Office.

"It's amazing how the press can link the two shootings together, when we've told them we haven't done so," Crompton expressed throwing one paper down angrily. He had just gotten his ear chewed off by Superintendent Matthews in a visit to his office.

"Why haven't we made a breakthrough yet? Surely these two killings are linked," Matthews demanded.

"Sir, we have found nothing to link them. One was in a pub car park, and the other was at an industrial estate. Yes, both were shootings, but that's all. The newspapers love to hype a story up to sell more, but they know squat. They're just guessing."

"Are we guessing? Have we got any leads? Matthews pressed.

"We're looking into some things which have cropped up. But its takes time as you well know. It's only been a few days. We've had no witnesses come forward."

"Yes, well. Keep me up to date with what's going on." With that Matthews turned on his heels and disappeared.

"Ok give me some good news," Crompton stated as he brought the office to order.

Lorimer began by filling everybody in on the visit to Jackson Davis's home, and the conversation with the neighbour.

"Now we know Davis went out between 9.30pm and 10pm on the night he died. We need to look at CCTV to see where he went and who he met."

"Right, as you found out about Davis, you can trawl through the CCTV images. We'd already asked for the discs covering last Wednesday and they arrived over the weekend. They're all yours," Crompton smiled.

"That's all right. I'm used to box set marathons. I watched the whole of Breaking Bad the other weekend," Lorimer laughed getting out of his chair. "Just remember to bring me lots of coffee."

HE REAPPEARED AFTER THREE HOURS OF LOOKING THROUGH THE CCTV pictures, looking like the cat that got the cream.

Crompton called them into a side room which had a large screen, so they could see the relevant pictures in greater detail.

"Where's the popcorn?" Monteith joked as they sat down.

"Shut up and concentrate," Crompton shot back. "Lorimer, the floor is yours."

"Thank you, Sir," Lorimer was at the computer down by the screen. "We know Davis left his house between 9.30 and

10pm last Wednesday night. That information we got from the neighbour. It was difficult tracking his car at first because of the dark colour, but thanks to the licence plate recognition system I have got more information."

The first few pictures showed Davis's car on the outskirts of the city travelling towards the industrial estate between 10.40 and 11pm. There was no CCTV near the industrial estate.

Monteith's phone went off.

"Just going to take this," he said getting out of his chair.

"No, you're not, sit down," Crompton was getting angry.

Lorimer continued. "The city centre pictures were difficult to pick out with the volume of traffic and not knowing where he was going. The first time we have him is on Crane Street heading into Bankside at 10.05pm." He put up the next picture. "The next time we see him was close to Austin Lane at 10.20pm."

"Austin Lane, interesting," Crompton sounded quizzical.

"I lost him for a time around this area, but I picked him up leaving and heading out of the city around 10.35pm." Lorimer put up the next picture and stood up. "If you look closer there is Davis, and there could be someone in the back of the car, but I can't be certain."

There was a black shape in the back, but it was unrecognisable.

"Thank you," Crompton walked down to the screen looking at the last picture.

"As you well know Austin Lane is the newest of the red light areas which are blighting this city. Davis looks like he has been visiting the area."

"You would have thought he would have kept his head down after being released. six months ago, and he's back at it again," Watson said

"He was just sticking two fingers up at the justice system.

Unsilent Grief

You will not change people like Davis."

"If he was done over by a pimp, or a prostitute, which would be some kind of justice," Monteith added looking at his phone. Crompton noticed.

"Well, we need to find out what happened around Austin Lane. Who did he meet? Did anybody see him or his car? Anyone fancy some overtime tonight over at Austin Lane? We need to do this before it starts to go cold. Monteith, my office now!"

Crompton led the way, shut the door after Monteith entered.

"What the hell was that?" Crompton was not happy. "I was waiting for a call," Monteith tried to explain.

"What? You think a personal call is more important that this investigation? More important to answer that call while we were going through information which could lead to a breakthrough?"

"Somebody slashed all the tyres on my car last night.

The call was from the garage."

"Whatever you have going on in your private life, you keep it separate from your work. Got it? Good. Get back out there, you're going to Austin Lane tonight."

Monteith stormed out and straight past Watson, out of the office. Watson joined him as he was calling the garage.

"Yes, yes, HOW MUCH!! You are joking. Ok I will pick it up later." Monteith turned round to see Watson. "£500 for four tyres, the robbing gits."

"Did you tell Crompton about what happened," Watson asked.

"Only about the tyres. Not about anything else. He made it perfectly clear not to mix private life with work."

"Right, get your head straight," Watsonsaid trying to calm Monteith down. "I'll drop you off to pick up your car and then let's get Austin Lane sorted. OK?"

When they came back into the office, things had developed even more. And not for the better.

"Right gather around," Crompton instructed. "Change of plan. Just got a phone call. We had another shooting, over at Bennington. Watson, Monteith, I want you to check that out. Mac and his team are already at the house. Here is the address. Lorimer, looks like I'm coming with you tonight to Austin Lane. Let's get going."

It was almost evening when they got to Bennington. Monteith had picked his car up, so they arrived separately. "Hope this doesn't take too long," Monteith grumbled. "Got some place to be? More important than this?"

Watson threw him a look.

The driveway of the house had already been taped off. Mac's morgue van and the crime scene vehicle were parked on it. The front door was covered with a forensic tent. They took paper shoes out of the box next to the door and slipped them over their own. Inside the house the forensics team was busy collecting possible clues.

Watson and Monteith went through into the main living room. A tent had been erected over the patio doors. More of the forensic team were taking photographs of the patio area and dusting for fingerprints.

"Mac?" Watson called out.

"In the kitchen," he answered

Walking into the kitchen they came across Mac crouched over the body. A male: in a pool of congealed and drying blood. An overturned chair lying nearby.

"Evening lads, we have to stop meeting like this," Mac sighed. "IC 1 male. Shot twice in the chest. Also suffered a beating, see these two wounds on the top of his head? Not found the weapon yet. I need to take him back to the morgue and get him cleaned up, so I can take a better look. "

"Was the attack in here or did it start elsewhere?" Monteith asked.

"In here. There are no blood trails or splatters anywhere else in the house we have seen."

"Do we have an ID?"

"The wife identified him. Adrian Knowles," Mac confirmed.

"Where is she now?" Watson asked.

"I believe she is next door with a neighbour. Police liaison officer is with her."

Monteith called Watson into the living room. "I think we may have a big problem."

He was looking at some of the personal pictures dotted around the room. Adrian Knowles was shaking hands with former Home Office ministers and local dignitaries. The pictures were taken at local and national meetings, some of which had national media coverage.

"Matthews is going to be in his element tomorrow when this hits the media," Watson said.

"If this is linked with the other two murders we are in big trouble keeping this quiet. The media are going to have a field day."

They spent the rest of the evening around at the neighbours with Mrs Knowles. She confirmed that she and her neighbour had been shopping in the morning. Adrian had told her he was going to work in the garden. They came back around 2 o'clock and found him in the kitchen dead.

No, they were not expecting visitors.

No, he had not been threatened.

As they were leaving the house, the local media presence had grown. The local police were keeping them well back behind the tape at the end of the road. Even so they were taking photographs of anything that moved and trying to interview anyone they saw.

A constable approached Watson and Monteith. He had been doing the house to house visits. Reading his notes, he told them that the owner of the second house was looking out of the bedroom window when she saw a red car leaving the avenue about 11 o'clock. She confirmed that it was not one of the neighbours cars.

She didn't know the make of it or see the registration number.

16

CROMPTON AND LORIMER, with two female PCs, were in Austin Lane trying to ask if anybody had seen Davis's RAV4 on the night of his killing.

They split into pairs, Crompton and a PC covering one side of the lane, Lorimer and the other PC on the opposite side. The PCs were in plain clothes for discretion. If they turned up in uniform, the locals would think it was a round up and the prostitutes would disappear into the shadows. They wanted to be in and out as quick as possible, depending on whether they got the information needed to crack Davis's murder.

Crompton and Lorimer left the PCs asking the questions showing each working girl a CCTV picture of Davis's car asking if they had seen it. They both stood back, observing the area and noting the comings and goings. After the first hour they ended up with nothing. Either the girls were not in the area on that night, or they didn't want to talk. Threatening them would be no use; it would just make them clam up and then, say they were being harassed.

They were just taking a break when a voice broke the silence.

"Little Kenny Crompton as I live and breathe. Looks like all of my Christmases and birthdays have arrived at once."

Crompton turned round and came face to face with a mature lady.

"My God, Angie McDonald, you're not still in this business? What is it, twenty-five years?"

"Don't be cheeky, twenty tops."

Angie was dressed in a tight fitting printed leopard skin top, showing all her curves. Knee-length leather skirt, calf length boots and dripping with gold jewellery. She laughed, flicking her black, shoulder length hair.

Crompton kissed her on both cheeks and commented favourably on her looks. Lorimer and the PCs looked stunned and tried not to stare.

"Don't worry I won't bite," Angie said tapping Lorimer on the cheek. They both explained that they knew each other from Crompton's time on the beat. He had helped Angie out of one or two sticky situations. In return Angie had kept her ear to the ground and passed on anything of interest to the police. She was around when Davis killed the two prostitutes. Both Angie knew personally. Now she was more of a mother figure to the new girls, teaching them the dos and don'ts of the business.

"What brings you down here? In need of some company?" Angie asked.

"Jackson Davis." Crompton watched Angie physically shiver at the mere mention of his name.

"What's that bastard done now?" Angie said with distaste.

"He is dead. Murdered."

"Good riddance," Angie cheered.

"Trouble is, he was down here on the night he was murdered." Crompton showed Angie the CCTV picture of Davis's car. "We came down to see if anyone remembers seeing it."

"That's his car?" Angie asked alarmed.

"Yes, Why?"

"I did hear there was an incident with one of the younger girls, Cherry."

A car pulled up across the road, a few yards down from where they were standing. A girl got out, giving the driver the finger and a lot of verbal abuse.

"That's Cherry," Angie pointed out. "Looks like she had trouble with a punter. Do you need to speak to her?"

"Yes. If she has information, we need to talk to her."

Angie crossed over to speak to Cherry first. After five minutes of what looked like a heated discussion with lots of head shaking and arm waving, Angie beckoned them over. She introduced them to Cherry, saying they were not here to cause trouble, but they thought she could have some information that could be helpful with their enquiries.

Cherry explained what happened on the night in question that Davis's car pulled over next to her. She was about to get in when somebody shoved her to the ground from behind. She didn't see the person, but while she was on the floor she heard shouting from inside the car.

"It was something like DRIVE NOW, and WHAT'S GOOD FOR YOU," Cherry tried to remember.

"The next thing a car door shut, and the car took off, spraying me with muck." She showed them the cuts and grazes she still had on her legs.

"Are you willing to come in and make a statement?" Lorimer asked.

Cherry violently shook her head and backed off. Angie touched her arm lightly trying to calm her down. They stepped away for a moment and spoke in hushed voices.

"I'll bring her down tomorrow for a statement," Angie said coming back to them. "She is young and naïve. She's had a hard upbringing. Will the afternoon be alright?"

"Yes thanks Angie." Crompton kissed her on the cheek again.

"Don't make it so long next time," Angie whispered in his ear.

"I won't."

17

Susan walked into the house after another tough day at work.

Working there was hard, not the first place she would have chosen but needs must. Family comes first, no matter what. She had to grow up fast after her mother was murdered. Her father fell apart before her eyes. Looking after him and trying to grow up as a normal child was hard. She had help from their next door neighbours, Mr. and Mrs. Banks. Mrs. Banks became more of a second mum to her. She was only ten when her world turned upside down. They made sure she wanted for nothing.

As she entered the front room, her father was slumped, snoring in his chair. An empty bottle of whiskey lying on the carpet next to chair.

How long had he been there drinking himself into oblivion? What happened? She would not get anything out of him now.

Susan went and took a shower, trying to wash all the foulness of her place of work off herself.

Drying herself off in front of the full length mirror, she stood and looked at her naked body. She still had all the curves in all the right places. At twenty years old, she should be out partying with friends and having fun with men. But she was stuck in a job she hated just to help her father out. Family comes first. She had been helping him for the last ten years, giving him all the love, she had.

Because of that, she had missed doing all the things her school friends had done. Now they were going to university, taking a year out and going travelling, or getting married and having families.

She had a boyfriend in the last year of school, Shaun. But it only lasted a couple of months, nothing serious but her father came first, and Shaun did not understand that.

She rubbed her body, looking at herself front and back. Cupping her small breasts, touching herself down between her legs wondering what it would feel like if a man did that. She lay down on the bed and brought herself to a frustrating orgasm.

Laying there she heard her father cough and splutter out of his alcoholic stupor. Sighing, she pulled on a pair of tracksuit bottoms and a T-shirt and ran downstairs to check on him. He was still slumped in the chair but had finally come around. Staring out of glazed eyes, trying to focus on the surrounding room.

She left him getting his head right and went to start their evening meal. Putting on the DAB radio to the local station while getting things ready. She stopped dead when the news came on.

"Reports are coming in of a shooting in the village of Bennington."

The newsreader, trying to add tension into his voice to emphases the seriousness of the report continued. "The name of the victim has not been released, but we are led to believe he is a prominent local man."

Susan did not need to be told who it was, she already knew it. And it explained why her father was in the state he was. She looked round to see him standing in the kitchen doorway. The eye contact between them was enough without words being said.

Tonight, was one for quiet reflection and family coming first.

WATSON ARRIVED BACK AT HOME LATE EVENING FROM Bennington.

The children were already in bed. Sally was busy at the table doing lesson planners. A half bottle of open wine by her arm. She looked up and smiled as he came into the kitchen. So not to disturb her, he blasted his dinner in the microwave, took a can of John Smith's out of the fridge and retreated into his den.

After switching on his computer, he put Eric Clapton's Slow Hand CD in the stereo. Something calm to listen to after the day he had. A couple of mouthfuls of dinner and a long swig of beer, the computer was ready. The online local newspaper was already reporting on the shooting in Bennington.

"Neighbours report that the dead man was Adrian Knowles, the former Governor at Claythorn Prison."

As they were coming away the T.V. news vans were turning up, giving the local police a headache. But that was for tomorrow Watson thought as he looked through the sports headlines.

He put Ronald Freeman's name in the search engine. Pages of information popped up within seconds. Pictures, newspaper reports, other documents including reports of the court case.

Since the internet became the so called go to place for information on whatever subject you are interested in, looking at historical and famous murder cases had become very easy. From Jack the Ripper to The Yorkshire Ripper. From Fred and Rosemary West, to Steve Wright the Ipswich Prostitutes Killer.

The local newspapers had set up excellent internet sites, scaling back their daily paper versions. Most of what Watson was looking at was from the local Ravenswood Telegraph internet site. Their lead reporter had done a superb job of recording everything. From the initial murder, to the police investigation, to the court case and sentencing.

Watson took his time looking through some of the information. Something caught his attention. "Detective Investigated" it said. He opened it and started reading. A smile turned into a broad grin as he continued. Watson opted to save the article in a folder, so he could look at it when he wasn't so tired.

Sally wandered in, glass of wine in her hand. "Tough day?"

"The worst and it will not get any better soon." He showed her the headlines.

Sally put her wine down and started massaging his shoulders, easing the tension in them. "Just relax," she told him.

"Relax when you're digging you fingers in that hard," Watson joked.

He took one of her hands kissed it and swung her around to face him. Moving her blouse up, he kissed her stomach. Sally played with his hair as he continued with the kissing.

Lay Down Sally came on the stereo, and Sally stood back laughing. "Good timing." She took off her blouse and skirt standing in just the briefest of bra and knickers.

"You want to see more, you will have to come upstairs."

She slowly walked out of the door to the stairs, giving Watson an eyeful of her pert bottom with just a string of knickers disappearing in-between her cheeks. Watson followed closely behind leaving Eric to sing to himself.

MONTEITH PULLED INTO HIS DRIVEWAY.

Getting out of the car he noticed a car going very slowly up the road. He stood as it drove closer.

"Nice set of new tyres you got there, pity to waste them," the passenger said out of the window laughing. The car sped off leaving Monteith cursing under his breath.

Katie opened the door in her dressing gown. "Who was that?"

"Just some morons looking for trouble, no-one to worry about." Monteith said moving passed her, putting his keys on the hall table and taking his jacket off.

"After this morning, I'm scared."

"There's no need to be."

Monteith took her head in his hands and kissed her on the forehead. "I'm going for a shower."

Monteith stood with the water flowing over him. Shaking.

He was scared too, and he hadn't a clue how he was going to get out

18

TUESDAY

THE NEXT MORNING, the Criminal Detective Agency's office was likened to a scene from DIY SOS.

New desks and new computers were being moved in to accommodate the influx of backroom staff Matthews had assigned to the Agency.

Matthews had gone overboard with things. The shooting of Adrian Knowles shifted things up a gear. No longer was it separate shootings of three people but they were dealing with a serial killer.

"So, tell me what we got before I go before the mass media of baying dogs out there?" Matthews was glancing out of the window looking down at the ranks of TV cameras, and reporters milling around.

Crompton sat behind his desk. Frustrated in having Matthews in his office, preventing him from getting on with his day job. He had always hated the politics of it. Policing was catching the criminals whatever it takes. He updated Matthews with the visit to Austin Lane and Knowles's death, giving him at least something to feed to the media downstairs.

Whether it satisfied Matthews, he could not care less.

With Matthews gone, Crompton called everyone into his office.

"I have just bullshitted the boss with a load to facts, so he can go and get mauled by the press out there. Officially we have a serial killer on the loose. That is not what we are telling the media, but that's what they will decide anyway. He will tell them something like 'Right now, we are exploring all avenues to catch the perpetrator of these heinous crimes.'

The TV in the corner of his office was tuned to BBC News, and it was taking the statement live. The volume was turned down low.

"So what have we got so far to solve these shootings?"

Watson took his eyes off the TV.

"Ballistics said the same gun was used in both the Freeman and Davis shootings. A Glock.22, very common firearm nowadays. We've also a partial fingerprint from the back of Davis's car, but nothing for a firm match from the database."

"We have one of the prostitutes from Austin Lane, who had a very lucky escape, coming in this afternoon to make a statement," Crompton added.

"I hear you bumped into a very old girlfriend last night, boss?" Monteith said with a mischievous smile.

"If you are looking for me to bite back at that comment…" Crompton stared back at him. "We believe now that Davis's assailant got into his car in Austin Lane and ordered him to drive away from there. Judging from the CCTV pictures, they went directly to the industrial estate. Hopefully, we can get a better description of him later today."

Crompton's mobile phone buzzed away on his desk.

He picked it up, looked at it and diverted the call. "What about Knowles?" He continued.

"Mac is doing the autopsy today," Watson continued. "Knowles was shot also, but he was hit over the head this time. Could be possible that whoever we are looking for is losing it? The first two killings were clinical, but this one was, I may be wrong, personal?"

Matthews had finished his media mauling, and the reporter was summing up.

"So, who are we looking for?" Lorimer put the question out to everyone. "A former prisoner with a huge grudge?"

"How many prisoners get released from Claythorn daily?" Monteith asked. "That's a lot of people to track down and interview."

"Can we cut that down? When were Freeman and Davis released from Claythorn?" Watson put another question into the mix.

"Can't remember but I will go and look now." Lorimer was already halfway out of the office to his desk.

Crompton's phone went off again. He picked it up, pressed a few keys and put it into his pocket.

"Can you lot work this out between yourselves for now. I have a meeting I need to be at." With that he got out of his chair, picked up his coat and made his way out of the office.

"What do you make of that?" Watson nudged Monteith.

"He's probably going to see that bird down at Austin Lane."

"I still think there is something he is not telling us." Watson was still curious.

"Are you still on about that? Just drop it and let's get on. Lorimer have you found out about Freeman and Davis's release dates?"

"Both were released in the last six months, Freeman first."

"When did Knowles retire as governor?" Watson asked.

"If I remember one of those photos we saw at his house was from a retirement party. I think it was about four months ago," Monteith tried to recollect.

"I can just about get my head around somebody taking out Freeman and Davis, but the ex-governor of the prison, seriously?" Lorimer said quizzical. "Whoever did that must know we would up our interest?"

"It depends on the killer's state of mind. If he is determined, it does not matter what we do. We might be dealing with a psychopath," Watson said.

"How did the killer know when Freeman and Davis were released? Knowles is easy; his picture was plastered all over the local papers announcing his retirement, and the new governor coming in," Monteith asked.

"Was he released around the same time as them? We need to ask Claythorn for a list of inmates who were released then."

"Lorimer can you ring Claythorn and see if we can get that information? Be interesting in seeing what comes back?"

"I will," he said picking up the phone.

19

DCI CROMPTON PARKED his car in front of the Dragon's Den.

This was one visit he did not want to make, but he had to. He knew the reception he would get; it was just whether he would be seen at all. He walked in through the front door and into the lounge side of the pub. The landlord Peter Preston was serving behind the bar.

Crompton ordered a half of bitter then asked, "Is Elizabeth around?"

"She is upstairs, who's after her?"

Crompton showed him his ID. "It's regarding her brother."

"Ok, I will see if she will come down, but after this morning's press I doubt you will get the friendliest of conversation. She had been drinking."

Crompton paid for his drink and sat down on one of the easy armchairs. He took out his phone and flicked through his messages. One from Watson, asking where he was and when he would be back.

"Look what the cat dragged in," Elizabeth said as she came into the lounge, full wineglass in hand.

"Hello to you too," Crompton replied. "You have a lovely

way with words." He waved his phone at Elizabeth. "I had to look up some of the words you used."

"Bastard."

"Now I know the meaning of that one, and I am sure I am not one of those. Now can we go somewhere private?"

"Upstairs. The lunchtime crowd will be in soon," Elizabeth barked, leaving Crompton in no doubt she was both pissed off and pissed.

She led Crompton through the kitchen and up a flight of stairs to the private flat above the pub. It was just a basic one which the industry provided its tenants.

"What do you want then?" Elizabeth turned to Crompton, arms folded.

"It was you who called me, remember?"

"Oh yes, when were you going to tell me about this so called, what did you call it, serial killer? I saw it on the TV this morning, just like that. No warning. Ronald's murder all out in public so everyone can..." her voice trailing off.

"We only worked it out this morning. It was my boss's idea to call the press conference. I had no say in the matter. I am sorry that you had to hear it that way, but I did not have the time to send anyone around beforehand." Crompton tried to keep his voice in a calm manner.

"Bullshit. You never gave my family the time of day when Ronald was sent down why would you care now?"

"Your father put pay to that. Because of Ronald's incarceration he threatened me and stopped me from seeing you."

"You could have stopped Roland from what he was going to do?"

"Yes, if I wanted my brains blown out. Nothing would stop him from committing that robbery. I had only just been promoted to detective. I tried to speak to him, but he said if I did anything to stop him, including calling in the police, both him and your father would make sure my time in the police would come to an end. If you get my drift!"

"I don't believe you. No, they wouldn't do that?" Elizabeth was incredulous.

"Believe me, they did," Crompton confirmed as he sat in an armchair opposite Elizabeth, who was nursing a large wine glass.

"Listen, I didn't come over here to drag over the past.

I came to update you on what's going on."

"Your boss beat you to that," Elizabeth said with disdain.

Crompton took a deep breath. "Also came to see if you or your husband had recalled anything from that night or even the days before. Sheila, over at your brother's flat, said he told you both he thought he was being followed."

"He was always saying things that made little sense. We took it he was struggling to take in all in after spending all that time in prison." Elizabeth got up and refilled her glass.

"What things did he say?" Crompton stood next to her.

He put a hand on her arm and spoke quietly. "It might help in our investigation."

Elizabeth took her time in answering, mulling things over.

"He said that he thought he was being followed." Thinking again she said, "Something about a red car hanging around."

"Did he mention make or model?"

"No. After the amount of time away, cars have changed a lot. I don't know half the cars around now never mind him."

"Where was this, did he say?"

"Outside the flat one time, then maybe when we were in town together. I don't remember."

"When was this?" Crompton started to write things down.

"Not sure now. Sheila might be able to remember better than me."

Elizabeth sank back into her chair, tears in her eyes.

Crompton knelt beside her.

"We will catch who did this, I promise. What you have told me today was good and it will help. We now have something to follow up on. I will see about going to see Sheila again."

"Thank you."

Elizabeth's voice was barely above a whisper.

20

CHERRY AND ANGIE arrived for their witness interview at the station.

Cherry dressed in a blue tracksuit and trainers. Angie on the other hand was dressed as outrageously as she was last night. Tight black leggings. A purple sequinned top over a bra which enhanced her large breasts leaving nothing to the imagination. A fake fur coat and sunglasses finished it off.

Cherry sat on one of the seats opposite the main desk while Angie approached the young officer at the desk.

"Angie McDonald here to see DCI Kenny Crompton." The officer looked up from his computer, straight into her buxom bosom, which the sight of seemed to affect his voice.

"I'm, I'm sorry, who? Who did you say you wanted to see?"

"That's a terrible stutter you have there. You should get that looked at." Angie laughed at the officer's embarrassment. "DCI Crompton; just say Angie McDonald his here."

"Right, ok," The officer tried to get his composure back before phoning upstairs.

Angie sat back with Cherry.

The desk officer came back. "DCI Crompton is out of the office at the moment, but DS Lorimer will be down shortly."

"Thank you, darling," Angie replied.

"I don't want to do this," Cherry suddenly said stood up and ran for the front doors, Angie quick as a flash caught up with her.

"Don't worry. I will be in there with you," Angie said stroking Cherry's arm then holding her hand guiding her back to the seats. "Listen, when I was your age the man whose car you were saved from getting into, killed two prostitutes. Those of us who were around at that time were scared. Some so scared did not want to help the police because they thought, if he found out they would be next. A couple of us thought differently and helped the police by keeping an eye out for him. Finally, they caught him. One of the girls he killed was my best friend. Therefore it's important for you to tell them what you saw, so we can get another killer off the streets."

Cherry nodded and put her head on Angie's shoulder.

LORIMER PUT THE PHONE DOWN AFTER SPEAKING TO THE DESK officer.

"Angie McDonald, the woman the boss knew from last night is downstairs with our witness. When's the boss back?"

"Don't know, he has not returned my call or text," Watson replied.

"This I must to see." Monteith went to get out of his chair.

"Down boy," Watson stopped him. "This is our sergeant's interview. Lorimer, bring them up here. You can do the interview in one of our offices. The ones downstairs might put off our witness from saying anything. We need to keep her relaxed."

Ten minutes later, they were in one of the side offices off

the main CDA office. Cherry and Angie McDonald on one side of the wooden table, Lorimer and a female PC on the other. Drinks had been asked for and served.

Lorimer started. "Thank you, Cherry for coming forward. We value your help. The criminal justice system cannot work without witnesses. They are the most important element in bringing offenders to justice. We believe the information you have can help in finding the killer of the driver whose car you almost got into the other night. The PC here will write down the conversation we have. You will then be able to read it over and make and changes that need to be made. First, I must ask this. Are you willing to make a police statement?"

Cherry looked at Angie for comfort. "Yes I am."

"I would like to take you back to last Wednesday night. Where were you and what were you doing?"

Cherry took a deep breath. "I was on Austin Lane, working."

"Can you tell us what happened that night?"

"I was standing waiting for another punter to turn up. A dark 4x4 pulled up next to me. The driver wound down the passenger window, and I went over to talk to him."

Lorimer put several CCTV photographs of Davis's car on the table for Cherry to see.

"Could you please look at these? Is this the car that pulled up next to you?"

Cherry picked the photos up one by one and studied them.

"Yes, this is the same car. I recognise the man driving it."

"Are you sure?"

"Yes, you never forget a face of a punter or the cars, especially the regular ones."

"Was this man a regular? Had you seen the car before?

Cherry hesitated. "Yes he had been around a couple of times before."

Lorimer glanced at the PC who was taking the statement down. "Have you got that?"

"Yes Sir."

"Now Cherry, can you tell us what happened next?" Lorimer was enjoying his first major investigation.

"As I said the passenger window was down. I walked over and leant on the door. I said something like, 'fancy a good night.'"

"So, you spoke first?"

"Yes."

"Did he say anything back?"

Cherry thought a moment. "It was... 'Get in and you will have the best night of your life'. You never forget a chat up line like that."

"What happened next? Did you get in the car?"

"No, didn't get the chance." Cherry took a gulp of her drink and looked at Angie.

"You're doing well." Angie rubbed Cherry's arm.

"I went to open the door, but the next thing I knew I was pushed hard away from the car and fell onto the floor. When I looked up someone was getting into the back of the car."

"Could you see who was in the back of the car?"

"No, not from where I was, I just heard the shouting."

"From inside the car?" Lorimer asked.

"Yes. The one who got in the car was shouting, 'Drive if you know what's good for you.'"

"You certain he said that?"

"Yes. He was banging on the back of the driver's seat shouting 'drive'. I sat up and went to move back to safety out of the way. I could see into the car before the door was shut."

"Could you see the face of whoever it was in the back?"

"No, he was turned away from the door." "What about his clothes?"

Cherry went into deep thought, trying to recall.

"There was not much light, but I did see brown or tan shoes, dark trousers and possibly a donkey jacket."

"Are you sure about what he was wearing?"

"Yes. Again, that is something we make sure we notice in case there is trouble with a punter."

Angie was nodding as if to add credence to what Cherry was saying.

"It's one of the first things we teach the newcomers. Know your punters."

Lorimer continued. "What happened next?"

"The back door was shut, and the car took off towards the city centre fast."

"It there anything else you can remember?"

Cherry took another slurp of the drink.

"I don't think so."

Lorimer looked at the PC who was finishing writing the statement.

"Right I will leave you for a few minutes. You can go over what the PC has written and if you think of anything else, we can add that to the statement before it's signed off."

Lorimer back into the main office headed straight to the coffee machine.

"What's she said?" Monteith was keen to get all the details.

Lorimer came and sat down near to Watson and Monteith.

"Well, she has confirmed Davis was at Austin Lane that night and a man got into the back of the car and threatened Davis. She could not see his face but had given us a description of his clothing. She is going over her statement now just in case she has missed anything."

"At least we have firmed up some of the thoughts we had prior to her coming in and added a couple of others." Watson went over to the information board looking at what they had.

The PC stuck her head out of the door and called to Lorimer.

Lorimer returned to the office and sat down.

"Right Cherry you've read the statement. Is it correct?"

"Yes, there is nothing else I can remember to add to it."

"If you remember anything else, please don't hesitate to get in touch with us. Here is my card, ok?"

Cherry nodded. Angie gave Cherry's shoulder a rub and gave her a smile as if to say you have done a good job. Lorimer continued. "I see you have already signed the statement and given your contact details. I think that's all for now. Thank you for coming in today." Lorimer stood up and shook both Cherry's and Angie's hands.

"Tell Kenny I am sorry I missed him," Angie said she left the room. "Bye boys." She added toward Watson and Monteith before she and Cherry were escorted out of the office.

"Bloody hell Karl, hoped she behaved herself in there.

Flaunting herself like that." Monteith said to Lorimer when they were out of sight.

"She was the model of decorum while she was in there," Lorimer said with a touch of upper class in his voice, which sent the office into hysterics.

"I trust you lot have got something of value to tell me, like we have caught the killer. Because if you have not why are we fooling around and not working?" Crompton had come in right at the end of the shenanigans.

"Sorry boss," Lorimer said as he went over to the board and updated it with what Cherry had said in the interview.

"Just interviewed the prostitute Cherry," Watson added "You've just missed your friend Angie McDonald."

"No, I haven't. I was accosted by her next to the lifts downstairs." Crompton was still wiping the lipstick off his cheeks as he came in and sat down at one desk. "What did Cherry give us?"

"A lot less than Angie gave you boss," Monteith said which sent the office into laughter again.

"Ok, ok, fun over. Point taken." Crompton said smiling, trying to get them back to some sort of order. "What did Cherry have to say?"

Lorimer went back over the statement, giving emphasis to the new bits of information.

"So, what have we got?" Crompton asked before running through the info on the board.

"The gun was the same one for the Freeman and Davis's shootings, and we are pending the Knowles autopsy so waiting for the gun used there. We have a witness giving us a partial identification of the killer from what she saw in Davis's car. And we have a possible sighting of a red car driving away from Knowles's house which did not belong there."

Crompton thought.

"That woman who looks after the building where Freeman was living. Didn't she say Freeman told her he was being followed?"

"Yes, but she and his sister put that down to paranoia." Watson reminded him.

"I know, but it might help to clarify it. There was a red car at Knowles's. There might be one at Freeman's flat? Watson, Monteith go and see her and check it out. Lorimer? Has the prison sent that list of released inmates through yet?"

Lorimer went over to his computer and searched his emails.

"It came in ten minutes ago. I'll make a start on this."

Crompton went into his office, followed by Watson. "Boss I tried to get hold of you when Angie turned up."

"I know, I got your messages." Crompton was looking straight at Watson.

"Thought you wanted to be here, that's all."

"I had important business to take care of. Lorimer sounded as if he was all right with the interview. No problems I should be aware of?"

"No, no. We will get off now."

Watson left the office confused thinking he had just missed something but could not put his finger on it.

21

MONTEITH PULLED out into traffic and headed towards Thelwell.

Watson was quiet in the passenger seat beside him. He put the car stereo on to break the silence.

"Old MacDonald had a farm, ei, ei, o," Monteith started singing.

"What the hell are you listening to?" Watson finally said something, but still staring out of his window.

"Oh, you are still living."

"Yes, but what the hell is that you have on?"

"Just one of Pixie's CDs. Thought we would have some music on!" Monteith said straight faced, bursting into song again, "With a quack-quack here and a quack-quack there."

Watson reached over and turned it off. "Ok grumpy what's up?"

"Don't know. I still think there is something that Crompton is not telling us."

"You still on about that."

Monteith shook his head. "If he has something to tell that we need to know, he will. Now we need to get more information on these killings. Get over it."

Just outside Thelwell they heard sirens. Monteith looked in his mirror and spotted blue lights coming up from behind fast. They pulled over with the traffic and watched two Volvo squad cars and a Volvo dog handling car flash by.

"Looks like somebody called for some taxis to take them into town." Watson grinned. Monteith burst out laughing.

A couple of minutes later Monteith pulled up outside Freeman's old flat. They noticed that there was nobody outside the shop across the road like the last visit.

"They must have gone to see which house the squad cars have been called to," Watson said getting out of the car.

They walked up to the door, knocked and when asked showed their ID to the camera. Sheila opened the door and led them into her office. It had been tidied up leaving them with more room to sit down.

"What can I do for you today, gentlemen? I trust it's about Ronald Freeman?"

Watson started. "When we were here before you mentioned about Ronald saying he was being followed. Can you help us on that? Did he say was it someone on foot or in a car?"

Sheila sat back and thought. "He mentioned nothing directly to me. It was something that Elizabeth commented on him saying."

"How about the others that work here? Could he have said something to them?"

"It's possible. Do you want to talk to them?" Sheila picked up a radio. "Mike, Steven, can you come to the office please?" Both answered that they were on their way.

"Are you any closer to catching who did this? I saw the news you are looking for a serial killer."

"Investigations are ongoing, which is why we are here." Watson informed her.

"Plus, you don't always believe what the media says." Monteith added. As he was saying it, his phone went off.

Taking it out, he looked at the text message shaking his head. He replied and put it away.

As they were talking, there was a knock on door and Mike and Steve walked in. They were in their painting overalls and looked like they had more on themselves then what they were painting. Following introductions, they all settled down.

Watson started with the questions.

"Did either of you two speak to Ronald in the weeks leading up to his killing?"

Mike spoke first. "Only in passing really. He tended to keep himself to himself. We took it to be a throwback from when he was in prison. He would say hello and mention if something needed checking in his flat, but nothing else."

Steve added, "Most of the time his sister Elizabeth was around with him."

"Did anything out of the ordinary happen during that time?"

"Like what?" Steve asked back.

"Well, we are looking into the possibility he was being followed. His sister said he told her he thought he was being followed. Did you see anybody or any cars around the front of here?" Monteith asked.

They looked at each other, and Mike finally spoke.

"He did come in one evening after spending the evening over at his sister's. He was as usual a bit worse for drink, but he looked very agitated. I asked him if he was all right and he took me outside. He pointed across the road as a car parked there moved off. He said it had followed him back from the pub."

"Did you get a good look at it?"

"At a guess, a red saloon. It was dark and with only the security lights from the front of here and the street lights to see by, it would be only a guess," Mike continued.

"Are you sure?" Watson pushed him. "As sure as I can be."

"Which way did it go when it left?"

"Back towards town. I ran down to the roadside when it moved off, but it was too far down the road to see anything else." Mike shrugged his shoulders. "That's all I can remember."

"Did you see it again after that?" Watson continued. "No, we all kept an eye out for it, but I don't think it has been back."

"Thanks for that lads, we will be in touch if we require anything else." Watson wound up the discussion.

Later as they were standing outside with Sheila, all the police cars which they saw earlier went past back to the station. A fourth police van had joined the estate clear out while they were in the office. One of the kids who usually hung out outside the shop walked passed.

"What's happened Kevin?" Sheila asked.

"The Claytons and the Edwards were having their usual fight over territory. Six arrests I heard this time. Par for the course."

"Should be entertaining back at headquarters tonight," Monteith exclaimed.

"Would not want to be the custody sergeant when they get booked in," Watson agreed as they got back into the car.

The trip back to the headquarters was slow due to the rush hour traffic. Watson noticed that Monteith was getting fidgety and stressed. Shouting at other drivers and sounding his horn a few times. At a roundabout, a white van from a local courier company cut in front of them, causing Monteith to brake abruptly followed by a volley of expletives through the open window at the driver.

"Calm down Keith. Shouting won't get us there any faster, even though that driver is a moron for doing that." Watson said loosening his grip on his seat and door handle.

"I need to get back and away from work, that's all," Monteith answered back sharply while looking at his watch.

"You on a promise from Katie?" Watson smiled. "What? No. What you on about?" Monteith's answer was short and too quick for Watson's liking.

"Right, what the hell is wrong with you? What is getting at you so much you are like a bear with a sore head?"

"Nothing is wrong with me," Monteith bit back. "If you don't want me to drive, you can always use your car. We always use my car."

"Where the hell did that come from? Did I say anything about your driving or your car?"

Monteith pulled into the headquarters car park and parked up in the only space available close to the main back door. So, Watson changed his tactic.

"Keith, what it the matter?" Watson's said in a more conciliatory approach.

"Nothing's the matter, get off my back will you."

With that Monteith jumped out and slammed his door, walking towards the back door without waiting. As Watson got out flabbergasted, Monteith locked the car and disappeared inside.

When Watson went inside, the custody suite sounded like a mix of feeding time at the zoo and a barroom brawl.

The Custody sergeant was losing his voice with having to shout above the noise, and he was close to losing his temper. Nine officers were trying to keep order between the Claytons and the Edwards family members who had been arrested earlier. The air was turned blue with threats from both families, and that was just from the women.

Watson headed for the door go upstairs when he heard his name being called.

"Mr. Watson, Mr. Watson."

It was Joseph Clayton, the head of the Clayton family. He was waving his walking cane to make sure Watson knew who was calling him.

"Joe, what are you doing here?" Watson walked over. "I thought there was a truce between you two?"

"Billy found out they were undercutting us on our merchandise and selling it on our part of the estate. He went over with a couple of his brothers to sort it out. I came down to try to smooth things over."

"Sorting it out, meaning they went over to teach them a lesson."

"You are putting words in my mouth Mr. Watson. Now that is not allowed." Mr. Clayton wagged a finger at him.

"I've got work to do. Good to see you Joe."

Watson turned to leave.

"Your partner seemed a bit angry when he came in before you?"

"Case were working on, nothing else."

"Oh, ok. Pass on my regards," Mr. Clayton said with a smile.

22

WEDNESDAY

Susan sat across the kitchen table from her father.

It had been two days since he killed Adrian Knowles and this was the first time since then he was not either in a drunken stupor or had a massive hangover. He had spent most of it in bed, or in the toilet being sick. When he had not reached the toilet, Susan had had to clear it up.

Not surprising, since he had downed nearly a whole bottle of whiskey on Monday.

Instead of leaving him on his own, she had rung in to work and said she had a migraine and would not be going in. It had been two years since he had been on a drinking bender. But confronting Knowles and killing him had sent him spiralling back there. Susan had emptied the house of all other alcohol, so her father could not be tempted again. She had to get control of the father and do it now. Family comes first.

She watched him tucking into a large fry up and a mug of tea. The first thing he had eaten in two days. Susan had tried to keep his fluids up with water while he was recovering, most of which ended up down the toilet.

She was not going to pry into what happened at

Knowles's house because she already knew the outcome from the news. The T.V., radio and papers were full of it, and the previous murders. Her father would tell her in his own good time.

"That was good and just hit the spot," Littlewood said putting down his knife and fork after finishing his fry up. He took a swig of tea.

"How bad was I?" Littlewood asked.

"Very. Don't you remember anything?" Susan said after taking a mouthful of her tea.

"Nothing, not since leaving Knowles's house." Littlewood's face was a blank.

It wasn't till after Susan filled him in on the missing two days he realised what killing Knowles has taken out of him. The others he could not give a damn over, but Knowles. He got up and came round to give her a hug.

"Thank you for looking after me. I don't know where I would be without you."

"You would already be in jail or buried with mum," Susan blurted slapping him angrily on the arm.

"Fair point, you've got me there." Littlewood put his arms up in mock surrender. He picked up the newspaper and read the front page.

"At least the police don't have anything on us yet."

"Yet being the operative word." Susan reminded him. "Getting caught now by making stupid mistakes is something we should avoid at all cost, especially after all the hard work we have put in."

Susan pulled the little red book out of her dressing gown pocket. "Fancy doing a bit of a spying?"

"What have you in mind?" Littlewood was curious.

The smell of bacon and sausage baps wafted around the office along with strong percolating coffee.

The best officers from the Criminal Detective Agency studied the list of recently released prisoners sent over from Claythorn. All two hundred and fifty-three of them!

"Welcome to the biggest game of Guess Who we have ever played," Monteith joked.

"Boss, are we really sure that the killer is an ex prisoner?" Watson asked.

"No, but it's something we need to either confirm or pass over. We cannot do that without going through this list. Someone might stand out. What are you thinking?"

"Well, if you are doing this, with the ex-governor being murdered, do we include people working at the prison now or previously worked there when he was there?" Watson mused. "Someone who is disgruntled?"

"I thought we are trying to reduce the suspects not increase them," a frustrated Monteith said

"How many people even work at the prison?"

"We are trying to reduce it, now can we get on," Crompton said.

Lorimer asked, "Why prison workers?"

"How does the killer know these people are ex-cons and are now out of prison? It has to be someone with the knowledge of the prison system."

"Obviously!" Monteith grunted.

"Could it have been an insider feeding information outside?"

"You and your theories. What proof have you got?" Crompton was getting frustrated.

"I just think we may be missing something if we only concentrate on released prisoners."

"Let's do this first and if nothing jumps out at us them we will look at the workers, ok?"

23

Jimmy Russell stood surveying everything before him; his domain.

Standing on the balcony overlooking the casino floor.

His casino. Lying on the outskirts of the city, it played host to the local wealthy and would be millionaires. Spending all their hard earned cash.

In his casino.

Russell came from humble beginnings. Born and raised on the Thelwell Estate, his parents were one of the first to move in to the new council estate back in the 1970's. His entrepreneurial skills showed up early at secondary school by selling sweets in the playground to the horror of the teachers. He got the cane. The pupil who grassed him up was found with a broken nose and a cut eye after Russell caught him on the way home.

After leaving school at 16, he joined his father and older brother in the car trade. Not the official car trade. The second hand, ask-no-questions-one. The no-one dares to complain, or they would find out how dangerous and viscous the Russell would be. Even in his early twenties he could appear to be charming but had a ruthless streak. If people said he couldn't do anything, he found a way. His way or a hospital visit. The end justifies the means. He never married, but there were always rumours of children he was supposed to have fathered.

He bought up failing local companies and turned them around in his own way, putting his own people in to run them. If a disgruntled employee did not like his ways, they would find themselves seriously injured or worse.

None of which could be traced back to Russell.

He became friends with councillors and the power brokers of the city. His first few millions came easily. If you were on the inside you were rewarded, but if you crossed him...

His older brother Allan came and stood beside him. "Sometimes Jimmy even you outdo yourself. Getting the council to agree the planning permission for this was a stroke of genius."

"It helps dear brother when you have something on the head of planning that he does not want to get out," Jimmy smiled at his brother.

Susan brought the coffees across to where Littlewood was seated in a well-known coffee establishment in the town centre.

They were lucky to get a table near the front window as it was getting near to lunch time. Already it was filling up with shoppers. Mothers with baby buggies blocking the way. Teenagers staring longingly into each other's eyes. Others staring at their iPhones as if their world would end if they did not keep up with the latest gossip. Office workers holding impromptu meetings in there because the works coffee was cheap and nasty.

Across the pedestrian precinct was a shop which was being fitted out. One fitter was Duncan Healey, released from

Claythorn five months ago after serving two years of a four year sentence for helping run a cannabis factory in a residential area. Inside he boasted how big he was working for a drug firm until he was introduced to the hospital wing by someone bigger.

"Interesting choice of subject," Littlewood commented to Susan as she put sugar in her cappuccino.

"I thought you would approve," Susan smiled back at him.

"Do you think you could do it?"

"Yes, I think this would be best if I took lead on this part of the project."

"But you have done your fair share already. Is everything set with the other subjects?"

"Yes, the letters went out to the clients the other day.

Nothing to worry about on that front."

"Have you worked out how you are going to tackle the subject?"

"I thought we could work that out together." "Sounds good to me."

AN HOUR AFTER THEY HAD STARTED THEY THOUGHT THEY WERE closer to finding a suspect from the list of released prisoners.

"How many are we down to now?" Monteith was pacing the office trying to get his legs to work.

"Ten," Lorimer called out. "Anybody stand out?"

"All of them, depending on what you are looking for.

Robbery, ABH, GBH, murder, extortion, drugs. This is a list to die for."

"Any of them who look good for our case?" Watson asked.

"Three of them are a good possibility. Robby Davison

Eleven years murder, Ian Smith four years ABH, and Billy Clayton five years GBH with intent.

"Billy Clayton! He was in the cells here last night."

Crompton looked at his watch. "They will be up at the court by now. You won't catch him there. Go and see what he says when he gets home. Before that, call in to see if Mac has done the autopsy on Adrian Knowles. Lorimer you can see what Davison has to say for himself."

Watson and Monteith arrived with Mac's music blaring as normal. This time it was Johnny Cash's Folsom Prison Blues. Mac was stripping off his scrubs after finishing Knowles's autopsy. His body, covered by a sheet, was being put into the mortuary's cold chamber by Mac's assistant.

"Hello lads, come for your next instalment of autopsy for beginners." Mac opened the bin and threw his scrubs in.

"No, just the findings please Mac. I don't think Keith's stomach could stand it," Watson chuckled.

"It's all right I will stand back here," Monteith was backing away to the other side of the room.

"This is not your normal music you play Mac?"

"I am playing it out of respect for our visitor," Mac said as he opened the cold chamber and pulled out Knowles's body.

"He was killed by two bullets to the chest." Mac pointed to the holes which were separated by the Y cut from the autopsy. "But it's this which is the interesting thing."

He showed Watson the deep cut to Knowles head just above the hairline at the front of his head.

"Whoever did this was acting with force, maybe even anger. Looking at the deep lacerations here and here, he was hit twice by his attacker. Did not find anything at the house which looked like it was used. So perhaps the assailant took it with him."

Watson looked closely at the wound.

"Would the butt of a hand gun cause that much damage?"

"Maybe? And from the angle of the wound I would say you are looking for a left handed attacker."

Mac nodded.

Watson turned to speak to Monteith, but he wasn't there. He asked Mac's assistant if he had seen where he went, but he shook his head.

"Looks like your partner has done a runner again," Mac exclaimed.

Watson ran out of the mortuary feeling frustrated with his partner. He stopped quickly. He could hear a one sided conversation.

"No Mr. Russell I hear what you are saying. I will try but... Yes, 8 o'clock tonight, I'll be there. Thank you, Mr. Russell. Goodbye."

Watson walked around the corner as Monteith was trying to put his phone away.

"There you are, what happened? You were there one minute, then you were gone." Watson tried to sound concerned.

Monteith turned quickly. "It's nothing, you know me and dead bodies in that place. Just feeling a bit queasy.

Watson patted him on his back. "Just as long as you are all right. Let's go and get back with what Mac has told us."

24

THE JOURNEY back into the Thelwell estate was this time uneventful.

At least Monteith put some suitable music on this time, Meatloaf's Bat Out of Hell.

"Remember when we went to see him in concert?" Monteith turned the volume up.

"Yep, what an excellent night. Even with the other halves present," Watson laughed. "We need to arrange a night out, just the four of us. Let our hair down. Old gits rule ok."

"Don't say that last part in front of your Sally. She will ban you from the bedroom," Monteith said, wagging a finger.

"Oh, and your Katie won't?"

"No, she will just ban me from the house," Monteith laughed back, and the both started singing along to the songs.

As they got closer to the estate, Monteith turned the music down.

"You still think we are barking up the wrong tree?" "Yes, I have a gut feeling we are."

"Is that the same gut feeling you have about Crompton and the Freeman murder? Something he is not telling us?"

"Exactly the same. I think someone on the inside is

feeding information out - when they're getting released or have been released - and where to find them now."

Monteith looked at Watson and shook his head.

"What are you suggesting? That they tell all the prisoners being released there is a psycho out there looking for ex-cons? I will tell you what will happen. Some of the hardened ones will say for them not to put anyone in their cell as they will be back for tea time after killing the bastard."

Watson shrugged his shoulders as Monteith continued his rant.

"And half the people on the Thelwell Estate are ex-cons or know someone who is. What do you want to do with them? Warn them? There will be vigilantes all over the estate gunning for trouble. It would make the feud between the Claytons and the Edwards look like a vicar's tea party."

"That remains to be seen, anyway eyes on the road as we are here."

Watson brought Monteith back to the matter at hand, as they reached the estate. Driving past the flats they had visited and the shop on the other side of the road, with the kids still outside. They followed the road around and turned off into one of the side streets. The Claytons' place was half way down. A semi-detached house, with a large front garden and driveway.

Monteith parked on the street. Curtains twitched in neighbouring houses. "Neighbourhood watch," Watson said, nudging Monteith as they walked up to the door. Joseph Clayton had seen them park and was already opening the door.

"Mr. Watson, Mr. Monteith. What a pleasant surprise. Please come in. We don't stand on ceremony here." Joseph stood leaning on his walking cane. His frail body underlined his years, but his mind was still very sharp.

"You go and sit down Joseph, I have the door." Watson

watched as the old man slowly walked back to his chair near the fireplace.

"I see the neighbourhood watch is alive and well," Monteith said as he was sitting down.

"Nosey buggers!" Joseph said back. "Wish they would all bugger off."

As they settled down with some small talk, a red battered Vauxhall Vectra pulled up the drive. Watson and Monteith looked at each other. Two men got out. They looked and gestured towards the BMW.

"That will be Davy bringing Billy back from court." Joseph said.

"You did not go? Watson enquired,

"No, I've seen enough of the inside of the County Court to last a lifetime. We are on first name terms with the judges down there."

The front door opened, and both men strode into the living room.

"Who the fuck parked their car outside out house?" Davy shouted, before he was aware that his father had company.

"Boys, you remember DS Watson and Monteith?" Joseph hissed.

"Oh sorry, didn't see you there," Davy apologised quickly.

"That's all right. We are here to talk to Billy." Watson was calm.

"What!" Billy exclaimed looking like he would lose his temper. "I've just been to court and you want to fit me up for something else, no way."

"Billy!" Joseph's voice was stern. "Shut up and sit down. Mr. Watson wants to ask you same questions about when you were in Claythorn.

"Why? That was years ago?" Billy sat on the arm of his father's chair.

"You have heard about the murders recently of ex- cons?

Well, you were in Claythorn at the same time as Freeman and Davis. Can you remember them?"

"You don't think I had anything to do with that!" Billy jumped up. "I don't do guns, no, no way."

"Calm down, we just want some information. Did you run into them while you were in there? Did they cause trouble while they were there?" Monteith tried to calm things down.

Billy sat back down.

"Davis and Freeman? Davis not much bit gobby; spent more time in the gym than anywhere else. Freeman was on my wing. Kept himself away from trouble, except for one time."

"What happened?" Watson asked.

"Don't know much, but he turned up one afternoon with a broken nose all taped up. Would not say what happened. The rumour was he was hit by a warden after saying something to him. Never found out the true story."

"There's fighting in prisons all the time. What made this stand out?"

"Yes there was, but they were prisoners who wanted to cause trouble. Wanted to be the ones with authority on the wings. Or those who were bored and took their frustration out by fighting. Didn't matter with who. Freeman was not like that."

"Can you recall the officer's name?" Watson was taking notes.

"No, not now it was so long ago." Billy shook his head.
"Now Billy, you realise I have to ask this as routine, where were you last Tuesday and Wednesday nights?"

"He was with me," Joseph jumped in seeing Billy getting tense again. "We were watching the European football on the T.V."

"Who was playing?"

"Man Utd beat Copenhagen 3-0 on Tuesday, and

Liverpool lost 3-2 at Inter Milan on Wednesday," Billy answered.

Watson looked at Monteith. "Well thank you for your help."

Back in the car Monteith turned to Watson while starting the car.

"You believe him not being out?"

"Not in a million years. He could have easily seen the scores on Sky Sport or the papers to cover himself. He might not be our murderer, but he was doing something else those nights and not watching football."

25

BACK AT THE office Watson and Monteith filled the others on what Mac and Billy Clayton had told them.

Lorimer had been to see Robby Davison. His ex-wife said they had split soon after he came out. He had been living somewhere in Spain for the last three years.

Crompton asked Watson and Monteith into his office. "I've had word that Freeman's funeral is tomorrow.

I want you two to go and keep an eye on it. See if anyone turns up that does not belong there, or anyone who we know, and we have not thought of."

"Babysitting a funeral?" Monteith said. "Surely we had better things to do."

"Don't piss me off Monteith. You do what I ask you to do ok?" Crompton rattled back. "It's at the cemetery at 10 o'clock and I want you there. Now get back to work."

When Monteith left the office, Watson closed the door behind him.

"Are you all right boss?" Watson was worried.

"What?" Crompton looked up from his paperwork."Yes, I'm ok."

He threw his pen back down on the desk and leaned back in his chair. "Matthews is on my back wanting a quick resolution to this horror show, and I cannot make him see we are doing all we can. Without a breakthrough, we're buggered."

Crompton looked washed out. His normal demeanour had gone, and he looked like he had the weight of the world on his shoulders.

"We will get this bastard," Watson tried to sound upbeat. "We have things to track. He will make a mistake and we will be there when it happens."

Crompton looked at Watson. "I wish I had your optimism because I don't see it."

"Don't be too hard on Monteith. He has things on his mind at the moment. I'll keep an eye on him."

Crompton did not seem to be listening as he had his eyes on his paperwork. Watson left the office closing the door slowly. Crompton looked up and sighed.

"What's all that about?" Monteith said when Watson came out.

"Nothing, he is getting grief from upstairs and is under the weather. Let's get out of here."

MONTEITH DROPPED OFF WATSON AT HIS HOME AROUND 7.30pm.

As he left, Watson noticed he did not go in the direction of his home but back into town. Quickly he ran in the house to retrieve his car keys. Sally looked up from the television at him wondering what was happening.

"I'll tell you later," Was all Watson could think of saying.

"Grab a Chinese on the way back for us. Kids have eaten." Sally shouted as he shut the front door.

He jumped into his car and tried to catch up to

Monteith, hoping he could do it by the traffic lights. It did not matter if he didn't, he knew where he would end up.

Watson parked out of sight when he arrived at the casino. He managed to get there just in time to see Monteith go inside. He locked up and strode inside keeping his eyes peeled for his partner.

The casino was not busy. People were playing on the fruit machines; some of the tables had players on. Two of the high paying machines paid out their jackpot. Screaming and cheering came from the players and those around them. He saw one of them just sitting on the floor in front of the machine watching the money falling into the tray.

Watson sat at the bar and asked for a glass of lemonade, looking around for Monteith. After a few minutes he spotted him on the balcony. He was walking along with a couple of security guards or bouncers, Watson could not work out who they were as they disappeared through some large wooden doors.

Monteith was shown into a large office. Jimmy Russell sat behind his ornate wooden desk looking at his computer and typing way. Monteith was roughly shoved down into a leather chair cross from Russell.

"Gentlemen, gentlemen, that's no way to treat our guest." Russell turned away from the computer. "Apologies please."

The two bouncers mumbled their apologies and moved back.

"Mr. Monteith glad you could join us. Would you like a drink?" Russell was acting his imperious best.

"No thank you I am driving."

"Oh, don't leave me drinking alone." Russell went across to his drinks cabinet and poured a whiskey and a glass of iced water. Putting the water in front of Monteith, Russell returned to his chair.

"I believe you have something for me?" Russell leaned forward.

Monteith reached in his jacket, pulled out a thick envelope, and lobbed it onto the desk.

"There's a grand in there. Would've been five hundred more but your goons slashed all four of my tyres."

"Did they? Well, I am sorry if they got carried away. I will speak to them later." Russell picked up the envelope and put it in his desk draw.

"You're not going to count it?"

"I trust you. But if you've short-changed me, well who knows what my boys could get up to after what happened to your car."

"Have you finished?" Monteith felt he needed to get out of there before his mouth got him into more trouble.

"Yes, I think our business is done for tonight. I will deduct the money from the interest payments. You still owe me five grand." Russell sneered at Monteith.

Monteith shot out of his chair towards Russell, but Russell's goons were faster grabbing and holding him.

"Oh, by the way, on your way out take your lapdog with you." Russell turned his computer screen around. On it were CCTV pictures. One was a close up of someone sitting at the bar. Watson.

Watson was looking round the casino floor when the whirlwind that was Monteith hit.

"OUTSIDE NOW!" Monteith growled as he walked by.

Just as they stepped outside, Monteith swung round and landed a right-handed punch to Watson's face which made him stagger back.

Watson grabbed hold of his face and winced not believing what his partner had just done.

"What the hell was that for?"

"Take your pick? Spying on me, letting Russell see you, not trusting me. Listening to my phone calls." Monteith was incandescent with rage.

"Well if you let me help with Russell and whatever trouble you are in, I would not have to."

"It's none of your business!" Monteith stormed off, started his car and flew out of the car park, leaving the casino's clientele running and diving out of his way for safety.

26

THURSDAY

The air was tense when Watson and Monteith arrived at the council cemetery just before the Freeman cortege.

Following last night's altercation, they arrived in their own cars, parking in the small car park at the front gates. Only official funeral cars and council vans being allowed into the cemetery. There were several cars already there, so it was a tight squeeze to get into the last places available.

Having been told beforehand which plot Freeman's last resting place would be, they sorted out a good vantage point overlooking the area, not too close but close enough. Neither of them wanted to start a conversation.

Egos took over.

They mumbled good morning as they took up their vantage point.

Just along from where they stood, a middle-aged man was tending to a grave of a loved one. They watched him clear the dead flowers and weeds way, putting fresh roses in their place. Kneeling, he touched the headstone and looked like he was saying something.

Freeman's cortege pulled in through the gates. A hearse, with two official cars and three other cars following. Slowly they made their way through to where the burial was to take place, parking close by. Elizabeth and her husband got out of the first car, with other family members alighting from the other cars.

Elizabeth looked around the cemetery. Watson and Monteith were unsure if she had seen them. Freeman's coffin was lifted from the hearse and carried by six pallbearers. The family following close behind to the grave side.

"The amount of funerals I have seen over the years."

The man who was tending the grave had moved next to Watson and Monteith. "Some big and flamboyant, some small family only ones."

"And this one?" Watson glanced at the man before focusing back to the funeral.

"Normal size. Looks like close family and friends. I take it you're not family?"

"No," Monteith replied, showing his ID card.

"Ah surveillance. Whose funeral are you interested in?"

"Ronald Freeman," Monteith said, looking with frustration at the man who disturbed them.

"Oh, I read about him in the local paper. Nasty stuff. Is his murder one of the ones that this serial killer you're after did?"

"Investigations are still ongoing sir. Now if you don't mind!" Monteith was getting pissed off with the interloper.

"Hope you catch him soon." With that the man moved off towards the entrance.

"Stupid bugger," Monteith mumbled under his breath. Watson looked at him and shook his head.

"What?" Monteith started to smirk.

Littlewood smiled to himself as he walked away from the two detectives. They stood out a mile. He knew whose funeral it was. He had spoken to the grave digger. It was just interesting to see the police detectives here watching.

What were they expecting to see or happen? The killer turns up? That only happens in films and TV series, right?

When the man was out of earshot Watson tried to get Monteith to talk about the previous evening's events, but he was in no mood to reciprocate. Monteith was in big trouble and would not or could not accept it. It reminded Watson of when Monteith went through the same gambling addiction which almost broke his marriage.

Then it was the horses.

Monteith was always found in the bookies when he was not on duty. And even when he was on duty, he wanted to know the results from that day.

Katie stood by him. They had only been married seven months, and she was pregnant with Rebecca. Monteith agreed to see Gamblers Anonymous and get counselling. It worked for a few years. But Watson could sense that this was much worse than back then.

With Jimmy Russell on the scene Monteith's gambling had exploded. You got involved with Jimmy Russell and nothing good came out of it. How had he got involved with Russell? Why was he behaving like he was?

Watson could not do this on his own. He needed help to help his buddy, his partner, his long-time friend.

27

FRIDAY

For the last day and a half everybody felt they were getting nowhere.

Banging their heads against a brick wall. No new leads were coming in but at least whoever this psycho was thankfully they had not killed again. Watson stared at the information they had collected on the board for what seemed the thousandth time. He could hear a phone ring.

What had they missed? Lorimer came and stood by him.

"Penny for them?"

"You'd need a pound coin for what's in here." "Only a pound?"

"I'll give you the first few for free."

Both tried to crack a smile but without success.

"The front desk has just rung. They have a Joseph Clayton wanting to speak to you."

"Thanks, Karl."

Watson took the stairs down to the reception as the lifts were out of order again. That was three times in the last six months. At least he was getting exercise out of it. He did not even get through the door into reception before he was accosted.

"Mr. Watson."

Joseph was waving his cane around making sure he was noticed in the busy reception area. An elderly lady was reporting her bag being snatched. A man reporting a builder's van for dangerous driving. Two homeless people, who were well known to the police, were sheltering from the heavy rain.

Watson sat down next to Joseph.

"What brings you down here in this bad weather?"

Joseph looked around the reception.

"Before I say anything, can we go somewhere out of the way?"

Watson agreed and went to look for an office not being used. One of the interview rooms was unoccupied, and he led Joseph into it.

"I hope you are not going to tape this conversation Mr. Watson?"

"Only if you have something you want to confess to."

Both men laughed as they sat down either side of the table.

"Now would I do a thing like that? No first I would like to apologies for abruptly ending your visit the other day. It wasn't good manners on my part."

"Don't worry about it. It's all water under the bridge," Watson said.

Joseph continued. "Secondly, I asked Billy to really think about that altercation between Freeman and that prison officer and try to remember his name. He said all he could remember was he had a name like Wood or Woods. They did not use first names unless you were chummy."

"And it was definitely a warden that gave him the broken nose?"

"Billy said that was what he heard, but like we said before rumours go around like wildfire. Most are not believed. But some end up being true."

The rain was still coming down hard as Watson showed

Joseph out before going back upstairs. The reception was quiet, even the homeless had been moved on. It was the smell the duty officer told Watson.

People were complaining.

Back in the deserted office Watson added what Joseph had told him onto the board and stood back. With it being a Friday and information dried up, everybody had taken the chance to have an early start to the weekend. He had not noticed Crompton coming out of his office.

"You still here Terry? I thought you had gone?"

"I could say the same thing to you, boss."

"So, what have we really got?" Crompton came over to the board. "We are looking for a man who wears a donkey jacket, dark trousers and brown or tan shoes. He drives a red car, is left-handed and is possibly called Wood or Woods.

"He also knows about the prison system and can handle a gun." Watson added.

"Come on, let's get out of here, we can't do anything else tonight."

"Is Matthews still giving you grief?"

"Why do you think I want to get out of here? He's still in has office and I don't want to get called up there at this time on a Friday. He thinks we should be here 24/7."

They walked down the stairs and out into the car park at the back of the headquarters, saying goodnight to the staff on duty and dodging the early weekend drunks being brought in by two vans. The rain had eased, but it was still drizzling.

"Talking of grief, you and Monteith are treading on egg shells around each other. Had a lovers' tiff?" Crompton asked as he got to his car.

"He's got a lot on his mind and I overstepped the mark the other day thinking I could help. But he went in off the deep end."

"Could I do anything? Talk to him privately?"

"I will leave that to you. Like I said, I tried and failed."

28

SATURDAY

WATSON HOPED the weekend would be relaxing, back to being a dad.

Chasing a serial killer and trying to keep Monteith alive was more than one detective could handle. Three children and a wife sounded like a better deal, less dangerous he thought.

Did he think less dangerous? Not when you are asleep in your bed, on your back, and your six-year-old daughter takes a flying leap on the bed and clobbers you in the privates.

Saturday morning was football morning with Simon. He played in midfield for Ryland under 14's and the team was doing very well in the league. Watson volunteered to run the line. Not because he wanted to, or it was his turn, but because he did not want to listen to the bickering from the side-line over the serial killer.

The parents of Simon's team knew he had something to do with the police, as he knew what their occupations were through general conversations before and after the matches. Nobody questioned him over the things he was working on, things in the newspapers or the local T.V. It was other spectators who watched the match from either the opposing team or who just came to watch were talking about it.

Most were alright, it was the theorists and police bashers he did not care for.

He didn't want to get into a slanging match putting them straight on the facts of the case. At least the linesman only got grief if he got an offside wrong.

That he could handle with a big grin and some banter.

If his children kept him sane, his wife, Sally, kept him grounded. Fifteen years of marriage helped. He had seen the marriages of other police officers and detectives disintegrate before they realised things were wrong. Monteith's was almost one of those before it started, but they managed to pull themselves back from the brink.

Yes, Watson and Sally had had rough patches, all marriages do.

After the football was the gardening. Tidying up the flower beds and cutting the grass. Rachael was doing her best to help out. Dressed in her red coat and red wellies, putting the weeds into her bucket and carrying them to the compost heap at the bottom of the garden. Both were dodging the flying football from Simon and Jason. Simon was teaching Jason some tricks and skills he had learnt during training.

It was different over at the Monteith's home. Life now was akin to a battlefield.

He had not spoken to Katie for days choosing to keep himself to himself, keeping thoughts of the mess he had got himself into in his head.

He usually got home late. Rebecca and Pixie were always asleep. Jackie was sometimes up waiting, but most nights she was asleep as well. When she was up, it usually ended up in an argument.

When they did talk, it was one way from Katie as Monteith could not bring himself to tell her the full story of what a deep cavernous hole he was in.

He knew he should do because it affected the whole family.

Their savings had been depleted, meaning the holiday they had booked to Spain might as well be cancelled. He didn't even know if he'd be around especially after Russell had finished with him.

Where was he going to get five grand? It would have been four grand, but for Russell taking the grand he had given an interest payment instead.

29

SUNDAY

Duncan Healey was never one of the big men while he was in Claythorn.

He was just a small cog in the big machine that is the drugs industry. It was his attitude while he was in there that bugged not only the wardens but other prisoners. He had only been taken on to look after a cannabis factory in a rented house, and he could not get that right. Caught in the act after coming out of the house one evening completely stoned as a police car was driving passed.

In prison he acted like he was Mr Big, that's until he was introduced to the real Mr Big in the drugs world. Two weeks on the hospital ward followed after he was found at the bottom of some stairs with a broken leg and a broken arm.

Now working for a shop fitter, he was trying to turn his life around. He had even started jogging through the parks and around the lakes of West Ravenswood. He had gone out early this morning on a route taking in the river and with few runners coming out this early he felt as if he was on his own, just him and his music on his i-Pod.

So, it was a surprise when he approached the bridge over the weir, there was another runner lying down. She was holding her ankle and crying. Duncan ran over switched off his music and knelt down.

"Can I help you?"

The runner tried to answer through her tears. "My ankle, I went over on it coming off the weir."

"May, I take a look?" Duncan smiled at her to try to put her at ease.

"Yes, but be careful."

"My name's Duncan." He straightened her leg, so he could look at the ankle properly.

"Susan and thank you for helping. I don't know what I would do if you hadn't come along."

"Does this hurt?" Duncan moved her foot slowly.

Susan winced. "On the outside of the ankle."

"There does not seem to be any swelling yet, but the sooner you get ice on it the better. Do you think you can stand on it?"

"I'll try. My car is parked the other side of the weir."

"You can't drive with that ankle!"

Duncan helped Susan up, letting her put her arm over his shoulder for balance.

"I'm not going to drive. I will phone my father, so he can pick me up."

They started to walk back slowly. Duncan's mind was racing. Coming to the aid of a beautiful woman dressed in black Lycra knee length shorts and a yellow tight fitting top under a blue tracksuit, all his birthdays had come at once. Also, he noticed was not wearing a ring on her finger. They were halfway across when he noticed a man coming towards them.

"What you doing with my daughter?" The man shouted.

Duncan was shocked as his head switched between the man and Susan.

"Dad, what are you doing here?"

"I said what are you doing with my daughter you piece of shit?"

He had started to walk quickly towards them.

"Dad, he's helping me. I hurt my ankle."

"Shut up. I was talking to this piece of crap."

Littlewood pushed Duncan away from Susan and pulled out his gun.

"Whoa take it easy I was only helping your daughter with her ankle. Tell him Susan."

Duncan was up against the bridge edge with a gun at his chest.

Susan stood there with a big smile on her face and waving at him.

"It's better now Duncan thank you."

"What's this...?"

"Message for your drug friends. Drugs kill."

With that Littlewood put two bullets in Duncan's chest. He and Susan then eased Duncan's body over the bridge edge and into the weir. The body disappeared under the fast flowing water.

Littlewood turned to Susan. "How's your ankle?"

She kissed him on the cheek. "Race you to the car and you will find out."

With that she took off leaving Littlewood laughing.

30

MONDAY

CROMPTON ARRIVED EARLY into the office, catching up on paperwork before being hit by the force that was Superintendent Grant Matthews.

Normally the big bosses were nowhere to be seen, dealing with overseeing strategy and police standards along with finance. Smoozing with local bigwigs and dignitaries and attending high grade meetings concerned with making the police better at what they do.

That is until things like serial killers are on the loose, and the bosses come running to get their faces on the T.V. and the newspapers. Then you can't get rid of them.

Crompton took his first look of the day at his emails. All one hundred and thirty seven of them. Most of them coming in over the weekend. nine of them from Matthews. The deletion button came in handy at this time of a morning, especially before he had two cups of strong coffee.

One email caught his attention. It was from a newspaper and titled, "Would you like to comment on this?"

Attached, a Media Player film clip. It was piece of security footage. Crompton looked closely at it. His anger rose as the clip continued as he saw what was developing. By the end his blood boiled. He emailed a reply asking where they got the clip from not expecting the answer, but he had to try.

Watson arrived just as Crompton had watched the clip for the third time trying to get his head around what he saw. He called Watson into his office and showed him the clip.

"Did they say where they got this from?"

"I am waiting for an answer, but you know what the papers are like for a story. What the hell was it about?"

"I think it's better coming from him than me." Watson held his hands up in mock surrender. "If he found out I have been talking, you might find one of us in A&E.

CROMPTON CALLED BOTH OF THEM IN LATER THAT MORNING.

He had turned his computer screen around so both could see, waiting until both were sat down. Watson was trying to look relaxed, Monteith was, well, just Monteith.

"A newspaper reporter has sent me a clip of CCTV from a couple of nights ago and has asked me to comment on it before it goes public. I wanted you to look at it before I do that."

He was silent for a moment before he pressed start.

It showed Monteith arriving at the casino and going inside, being met by a pair of suited and booted security guards. They disappeared upstairs and through a pair of big wooden doors. The CCTV then switched to Watson sitting at the bar drinking and looking around. Next was Monteith striding towards Watson and both leaving the casino. The last shot was of Monteith punching Watson and speeding off.

When the clip finished Crompton sat back and waited for someone to say something. Watson was sat still, but he could tell that Monteith was about to blow.

"Care to explain?"

"No, it's none of your business," Monteith shouted. With

that he reached for the door and opened it. "Monteith, if you set foot out of this office without explaining yourself I will suspend you and Matthews will have to get involved. Now get back here and sit down. Whatever the problem it will not go away if you behave like a spoilt brat who has got his fingers caught in the till."

For the next hour Monteith spilled everything out regarding Jimmy Russell, knowing he could not continue.

He needed help and fast. He started going to the casino about six months ago with some mates. It started out as a bit of fun playing on the slot machines and Black Jack. During these visits he slowly lost control, betting more.

His friends tried to curtail him but soon realised they were out of their depth. Monteith then said he had met Jimmy Russell one night in the casino. They started talking and the upshot of that conversation was he was introduced into the big league. Starting with invite-only small stakes poker which took place in rooms at the back of the casino. Monteith said he did well during that, winning more than losing.

By that time his gambling habit was at its height and Russell let him sit in on some of the high stakes games.

Winning was becoming the normal, coming away some nights up to three grand up.

But then it started to go wrong.

At the end he owed Russell five grand. Russell banned him from the tables until the debt was paid. To add to the incentive, Russell sent his goons round to slash his tyres on the BMW.

Monteith continued, "The night the CCTV was taken, I had gone to pay off a grand of the debt. Russell said he would take it at an interest payment and I still owed the five grand. I did not know Watson had followed me, which is why I reacted the way you saw."

When Monteith finished, he looked drained.

"So, we can take it Russell leaked the CCTV pictures to the

paper." Watson added. "To make us see he can do what he wants."

Crompton sat contemplating what he had just been told. He could rant and rave about how stupid Monteith had been, but what good would that do? Send him in off the deep end and lose a good detective in the middle of a major crime? He had probably been through the wringer both at home and with Watson. Monteith knew what he was getting himself into when he started gambling again.

"When does Russell want his five grand you owe him?"

Monteith already looked like a beaten man but managed an answer,

"You know Russell, he always wants things straight away or else."

"I will have to tell Matthews about this especially as the papers have got hold of it."

"I'm dead anyway, what's another knife in my back going to do."

31

LORIMER WAS UPDATING the information board when they appeared out of Crompton's office.

He wrote three names, Gerrard Wood, Peter Woods and Colin Littlewood, and then turned to the others in the office.

"Just got off the phone to Claythorn. I was following up on what Mr Clayton had said about Freeman's altercation with a warden. They couldn't confirm that the incident took place because there are so many fights and beatings in there, like all prisons, it's difficult to track down one from that long ago. But they gave me the names of three wardens who were around then with Wood in their surname. All were working there when Freeman, Davis and Knowles were there. Claythorn are sending over what they have on record for the three."

"This won't be a wild goose chase?" Monteith tried to get involved but was still subdued after the grilling he had just taken.

"Sorry, but not all killers hand themselves in to police, some we have to catch." Watson sarcastically said looking over at Monteith.

"Ha bloody ha."

With that Monteith stormed out of the office, leaving everyone else staring at each other.

"Who upset him?" Lorimer said quizzical.

"Family troubles, nothing to worry about." Crompton answered. "Right, when we get the info from Claythorn we need to track down these three and see what they have to say."

Lorimer went back to his desk. "That's just come in. It includes last known addresses."

"Watson find Monteith wherever he has gone and you two can go and interview Colin Littlewood. Lorimer, you and I will visit Peter Woods."

Monteith was outside pacing around the car park cursing to himself. Looking up, he saw Watson coming out of the door and across.

"I'm finished, you know that. Screwed. If he tells Matthews about this I am out of here. You know what a straight down the line, by the book officer he is."

He slammed his fist down on the roof of his BMW leaving a slight dent. "Bollocks."

"They won't get rid of you. They need you too much."

"Oh yes, says who? Lorimer is gunning for his promotion. Why not get rid of the embarrassment and promote Lorimer?"

"You forget I was in that CCTV, they get rid of you they'll have to let me go."

"No, they won't." Monteith was shouting at Watson causing the other users of the car park to turn and look. "You'll just go down to desk duty for the uniforms."

"Why don't to listen to yourself. You're not the first officer to have a gambling problem and you're not going to be the last."

"Yes, but I bet none of them owe it to the biggest lunatic in the city. If Matthews doesn't get me, Russell will. I cannot pay him off; like I said, I'M SCREWED."

"Calm down, we have to go and visit Colin Littlewood and see what cock and bull story he has to tell."

32

THEY TOOK the long route to Littlewood's house so Monteith could calm down.

The silence in the car was deafening.

After parking on the street, they walked up the drive past a white Renault and knocked on Littlewood's front door. There was no answer so Watson knocked again while Monteith looked through the front window into the living room.

"They have gone on holiday."

The woman from next door was standing on her door step.

"Do you know where Mrs.?" Watson asked as he approached her, showing his ID. Monteith followed with his ID out. The woman looked at their IDs before answering.

"Mrs. Banks. And no, I don't know where they went. We came down for breakfast this morning and there was a note through the door from Colin saying they had gone away for a few days.

"Do they often disappear like this?"

"No. I cannot remember the last time they went away for a holiday or even a weekend. Why do you want to know?"

"We would like to talk to Mr. Littlewood regarding our enquiries. Have you known the family long?"

"Ever since they moved here twenty odd years ago. Very nice family."

As she was talking, Mr. Banks returned from taking their dog for its walk. Both Watson and Monteith showed their IDs again.

"Morning officers," Mr. Banks said.

"They're asking about Colin." Mrs. Banks updated her husband on the conversation.

"Well, don't stand on the door step, come in."

Mr. Banks ushered the detectives past his wife, who gave him a look of disgust.

They all went into the living room and sat down. Monteith and Watson on the sofa, Mr. Banks in his chair, with Mrs. Banks hovering around not happy that the detectives had been invited in. She did not like visitor's full stop.

"So, you want to know about Colin?" Mr. Banks asked.

"Your wife said you have known him for about twenty years?" Monteith started.

"Yes. Colin and his wife Jackie moved in next door about then. Very nice couple. She was pregnant with their daughter Susan at the time."

"And what was his job?"

"He had just started working at Claythorn Prison."

It suddenly dawned on Mr. Banks why they were looking for Colin Littlewood.

"You don't think he is involved in all these killings are you. No way, not Colin. He's not been in a fit state to do anything over the last few years. Not since his wife was murdered ten years ago."

Watson and Monteith looked at each other. This was new information.

"What happened with his wife?" Watson asked quizzically.

"You don't know? She was pushed down the stairs at home by two burglars when she confronted them. He was at work when it happened. Jackie died in hospital. After that he went to pieces, depression, and alcoholism. Lost his job at the prison. My wife looked after Susan as she was growing up because he couldn't. If you think he is involved in all these killings, you are wrong. He hardly goes out. The only time he does it's with Susan, or to the cemetery to put flowers on Jackie's grave."

Mr. Banks was getting furious.

"I tell you something. When he heard about that governor of the prison being murdered he was so upset over it, Susan told me he drunk himself into a stupor not wanting to believe it. Is that someone who could murder someone? Tell me?"

Mrs. Banks came over to soothe her husband. An asthma coughing fit took over his body. She gave him his Ventolin.

Watson and Monteith let Mr. Banks calm down before continuing. Monteith made sure he was ok before he continued.

"You said he lost his job at the prison after his wife died, do you remember why?"

Mr. Banks leant back in his chair bolstered by cushions.

"Something about a prisoner goading him over losing Jackie, Colin snapped and hit him. That was enough for the prison to get rid of him. He was not well at that time. Losing Jackie hit him very hard and he could not cope with the depression and he hit the bottle. We brought Susan up more than he did during that time. Helped her with her homework, took her in to sleep over when he could not look after himself never mind Susan. Saw her turn from a girl to a lady then to a woman. Social Services got involved and wanted to put Susan up for care, but because we said we could help she stayed, thank God. Losing Susan would have just finished him."

As Mrs. Banks showed them to the door Monteith asked

where Mrs. Littlewood was buried. She confirmed it was in the local cemetery.

Walking back to the car Watson said what they were both thinking.

"We've met Colin Littlewood already."

They rushed to the cemetery and to the place where they were stood for Freeman's burial. They found Jackie Littlewood's headstone.

"It was him. We spoke to him." Watson was frustrated. "He knew why we were here; he knew Freeman was being buried that day the bastard." Monteith was going spare.

Watson read the inscription on her headstone.

Her Life A Beautiful Memory Her Absence A Silent Grief

"This is more like unsilent grief," Watson said to himself.

33

Dumping the Skoda after renting a 4x4 under her mother's maiden name before taking off was a great idea of her father's.

They left it in a supermarket car park, unlocked with keys in the driver's footwell, while getting supplies. It would soon be spotted, but they would be long gone before that happened.

An hour later they pulled into the woodland holiday park.

Susan had booked a log cabin deep in the woods for a week. They would not be staying for that long, just a couple of days. Things needed to be gone through and set out. If they had done it at home, they might be disturbed by their nosy neighbours.

The Banks's were a lovely couple, and both she and her father had been indebted to them when her mother was murdered helping with bringing her up, but sometimes they were a pain. Spending time away would help in rejuvenating both of them.

No one to bother them.

Susan and her father unpacked and stood on the sundeck with a soft drink taking in the surrounding scenery. No cabin could be seen by any another. The local ducks were wandering around as if they owned the place, organising themselves into raiding parties knowing that they could be fed very nicely from the visitors. Susan spotted a couple of squirrels scurrying up and down a tree playing and looking for food and pointed them out to her father who smiled and had a little chuckle. Something he had not done for a long time.

The wood was full of birds chirping and squawking, seeing who could do it the loudest. Littlewood sat back on one of the wooden chairs on the decking and closed his eyes, taking in the sun. Susan sipping her drink leant against the fence which surrounded the decking, looked at him and smiled. The contentment on his face was a joy to see.

"Family comes first," Susan said to herself.

34

"You are sure we have got this correct?"

Matthews was grilling the detectives. Two pictures of Colin Littlewood and his daughter Susan had been attached to the information board.

"Yes, we're positive Colin Littlewood is the killer of Freeman, Davis and Knowles." Crompton said, "He killed Freeman because he had a run in with him in Claythorn. Littlewood bust his nose because of what he said about his wife's death. Also, because of why Freeman was in prison. He even turned up at Freeman's funeral; we even spoke to him not knowing what we know now. Knowles because he was Littlewood's boss who sacked him even after all he had been through. And Davis, for what he had been in prison for. Could have been shooting his mouth off while he was in there. Getting revenge for what he had to put up with while he was a warden, type of vigilante killing."

"Pity we can't let him continue." Monteith let out a sigh. "I know, bad taste," he added when everyone looked at him. "But it's what most of the public think. Prison is too good for some of these creeps. Davis was the biggest one of these."

"Do we know who killed Littlewood's wife and are they still inside?" Matthews continued.

"We are checking that with the prison now, but they have not got back to us as yet," Lorimer chipped in.

"Press them for an answer now, it's imperative we know for their safety," Crompton stated. "If they are out we need to find them and either warn them or protect them."

The phone rang, and Lorimer answered it.

"Yes… where? Are you sure it's his? Thank you, can you hang on? That was the squad room. They have stopped Littlewood's car for speeding in the town centre. Asked what you want them to do next?"

"Hold them and we will be there ASAP." Watson and Monteith grabbed their jackets and ran towards the door.

"Text us the position, will you?" Monteith shouted back.

Within ten minutes they had pulled up behind the squad car.

"They're still in the car." A uniformed officer commented as they walked up. "He's failed a breath test and there is a strong smell of cannabis."

Watson and Monteith looked at each other as they approached the car. Watson knocked on the driver's side window. It was wound down, but the driver was not Littlewood. In the seat was a thin, haggard looking man, stinking of alcohol and cannabis. Beside him a young girl who also looked as if drugs and drink ruled her life.

"Can I help you, officer?" The man slurred his words so much it was hard to understand.

"Is this your car sir?" Watson, pissed off that it was not Littlewood, tried to keep his calm.

"Yes, it's my car. We have just been shopping. I have just told the officer that." The man replied matter-of-factly. There were Tesco shopping bags on the back seat. Cans of beer had spilt out and a bottle of vodka could clearly be seen through one of the bags.

"Can I see your driving license, please?"

"Err. I must have left it at home. I can bring it around later?"

Watson had had enough. He told the officers to arrest them and they would be dealt with back at the station.

BACK THERE, LORIMER KNOCKED ON CROMPTON'S OFFICE DOOR. He was in there talking to Matthews.

He waved Lorimer in as he shut a file down on his computer. Lorimer filled them in on the information he had received.

"Just heard from the prison. Littlewood's wife's killers Andrew McNulty and Thomas Smith are still there. But they are due to be released soon."

"Do we know when?" Matthews asked

"No. They refused to give that info to a mere junior like me. Something about data protection?"

"Give me the phone number. I'll rattle their cage."

Crompton took the piece of paper Lorimer was holding. "Any news from the daring duo?"

"It was Littlewood's car, but it was stolen from a supermarket by a couple of druggies. Uniform is bringing them in now."

After a couple of nods Lorimer shut the door. Crompton opened the bottom draw of his desk, bringing out a bottle of Whiskey and two glasses.

"Bit early Kenneth, for this?" Matthews raised his bushy eyebrows.

"Only medicinal."

Crompton pushed a glass across the table. Matthews took it, swirled the scotch around and took a sip. "Yes, I agree, just medicinal."

"So, what are we going to do with Monteith?"

Crompton eased his chair back and came round to sit next to Matthews.

"Besides shoot him for being a moron."

"Well I hadn't thought of that, but that could be arranged."

"Joking aside," Matthews said, "I'll deal with the newspaper. I know the editor. When he is made aware that certain doors will be closed if they run this casino story, I think he will change his mind. As for Monteith," he looked at the contents of his glass. "Could we use him to get Jimmy Russell?"

"You want to use Monteith as bait, go undercover?"

"Not so much undercover. He already knows Russell. If he could get closer?"

"I don't know if he is close to Russell, he owes him money, but he is not friendly with him."

"Maybe it's time for him to get closer?" "And the five grand he owes?"

"We will give it to him to soften the deal. Say it was operational expenses to the finance department."

"Do you honestly believe he will go for it?"

"Don't give him a choice if he wants to continue as a detective."

Matthews looked at Crompton with a knowing smile as he got up out of his chair.

"Well if that's all, I have to sort some things upstairs. By the way that whiskey is very good; we must be paying you too much if you can afford that."

Matthews was leaving Crompton's office as Watson and Monteith got back in. They were pissed off because of what happened with Littlewood's car.

"He's done a runner. The bastard's done a runner." Watson threw his jacket down.

"He's dumped his car and is laughing at us because we cannot catch him." Watson's frustration was boiling over.

Matthews stopped by his desk.

"Anything caught on CCTV at the supermarket?"

"No, that's where we have just been. You can see Littlewood park up his car and go into the supermarket, but we lose him in the crowd. Don't know where he went after coming out. If he got into another vehicle waiting for him, we did not see him."

Watson was grabbing a drink and something to eat as he filled Matthews in.

Monteith continued, slumped in his chair.

"His daughter's car was still on the driveway when we interviewed the next door neighbour, so they are not using that one. They must have got another from somewhere. A rental?"

Matthews just nodded his head,

"Ok good work, keep me updated, thank you."

With that he left the office. Monteith and Watson just stood looking at each other wondering what just happened.

Matthews rarely spoke to them directly unless he had to, never mind give out compliments.

35

TUESDAY

ONE OF THE things detectives hate is early morning call outs.

Another is early morning calls when it's raining, and this morning at 6 a.m. it was raining hard. A call had come in from a dog walking insomniac at 5 a.m. who had been walking along the river near the weir. He had spotted something tangled in the undergrowth overhanging the river. The police divers were bringing the body to the riverside half a mile from the weir. With the rain the river level had risen, and the weir was flowing fast.

Watson and Monteith stood on the riverside in waterproof macs and wellingtons under the bright lights of the arc lamps looking like two drowned rats. Neither wanting to be there. After finally dragging the body out of the river and on to a sheet of plastic on the grassy river bank, they could get a better look at the macabre state of it. Mac was there to give it a once over before the trip back to the morgue.

"I can't do a lot at the moment with the body because of the bloating. I have to wait until the air and methane gas come out before I can start on the process. What I can say with any certainty is our body is male, that's it."

Monteith had had enough,

"So, you cannot give us how he died or when?"

"No, as I said not until the post mortem. Bodies in water react differently during decomposition which makes timelines difficult to work out."

Mac had started taking photos of the body. It still had its running shirt, shorts and trainers on. But because of the bloating they were very tight. Mac turned to his assistants once he had finished.

"Ok, you can bag him up." He walked back to the weir with Watson and Monteith.

"Sorry boys, I can't be more helpful at the moment."

"Don't worry, looks like an accident anyway, slipped in caught by the current, drowned." Monteith talked as if it was not worth their time.

"Thank you Doctor Monteith," Mac said sarcastically. "Maybe you can do the post mortem with me. I value your expert opinion?"

Mac looked at Watson who was trying not to laugh. "No bleeding way. I'll leave that to you." Monteith was shaking his head.

Mac and Watson burst out laughing. When the Mickey taking calmed down Watson looked around taking in the surrounding area.

"If he did not go in where we found the body, where did he fall in?"

"Judging from the flow of the river, anywhere from the weir downwards? But that is for you to work out. I only do the bodies," Mac replied.

Crompton was waiting for them when they got into the office later that morning. He was speaking animatedly to Lorimer over something, who was updating the board with photographs and details.

"It's nice of you to join us! Did you have a good early morning walk by the river?" Crompton joked.

"Oh, it was lovely boss, you should have joined us.

Walking in the rain with the ones you love," Watson said while staring longingly at Monteith.

"Well, Terry you say the nicest things."

Monteith acted like a love struck teenager and batted his eyes back at Watson while giving him a peck on the cheek. They both skipped hand in hand over to information board.

"So, the Secret Policeman's Ball is alive and well then," Crompton said, trying not to laugh. "Listen, we have some new information. I would like to introduce you to Andrew McNulty and Thomas Smith."

He was pointing to the new photos on the board.

"These two lovely people killed Littlewood's wife, and are due to be released from Claythorn this Friday. Now we need to be there before Littlewood and put them into protective custody until we catch him. I can't stress enough that we need to get this right. I don't want this bastard killing anyone else let alone these two. He's been one step ahead of us but now we can stop him. I have spoken to the governor of Claythorn and arranged for McNulty and Smith to be handed over to us before they leave. I want all three of you to take an unmarked Range Rover and pick them up on Friday and bring them back here."

"Have we any idea where he is now?" Watson asked.

Lorimer filled them in.

"No, looks like he has gone to ground somewhere. After ditching his car and leaving his daughters at home, we don't know what they are driving now. All rental places we have talked to don't recognise him and have no record of a Littlewood renting a car."

Crompton continued. "An APB has been put out already, so we should get word as soon as he is sighted."

Crompton's phone started to ring, he went to answer it.

"So, when are you two moving in together?" Lorimer said mischievously.

"When our divorces come through sweetheart, sorry."

Monteith went to kiss him but Lorimer moved quickly away.

Crompton came back over.

"Right, Lorimer. Can you organise that Range Rover for Friday with the car pool. You two, Matthews wants to see us now in his office."

"In his office? What for?" Watson was quizzical. Crompton's look back at him was withering.

"Oh right," Watson mumbled.

They walked along the corridor and into Matthews's outer office. His P.A. just stared at them over her glasses with a face that looked like she was sucking a lemon.

"Go straight in, he's expecting you."

Only section heads were called into the superintendent's office. For lesser mortals of the police service to be called in there was either for awards being given out, or for disciplinary reasons, as far as Watson and Monteith knew. Which one of these it was they didn't know.

Matthews was sitting behind his large desk typing away on his computer. To his left was a bookcase which stretched the length of the wall. It contained not only books but also files and personal items. In front of the desk were three leather backed wooden chairs.

"Be seated, I won't be a minute."

The three of them sat down not saying anything. It was akin to being called into the headmaster's office. Matthews finished and turned to address them.

"Right gentlemen, following your little escapade to the casino the other night, and yes Mr. Watson and Mr. Monteith I have seen the CCTV clip, I have managed to hopefully put out the fire."

Monteith went to speak but Matthews stopped him in his tracks.

"Don't thank me now because there will be repercussions. I have spoken to the editor of the newspaper and the story will not be run either online or in the paper. Detective Watson, now I know the full facts and you were only there because you wanted to keep an eye on your partner and nothing else, you can go back to the office.

"I would like to stay if you don't mind sir. Yes, he is my partner but also he is a good friend." Watson stood firm looking at Monteith.

"Very well, as long as you are ok with it?" Matthews looked at Monteith who nodded he was.

"As for you DS Monteith I have a good mind to demote you back to walking the beat because of this, but thanks to the intervention of both DS Watson and DCI Crompton I have been talked out of it. I am, however, putting a record of this on you file."

"Thank you, sir," Monteith mumbled even though he felt like telling them all where to go, and it had nothing to do with them. But he could not do that as it would probably lead to him being sacked for gross misconduct.

Matthews continued. "Well like I said there will be repercussions regarding this. Jimmy Russell as we all know is one of the biggest crooks around here. But we have never had a chance to get a sniff of him never mind get close to him. Until now."

Monteith was starting to feel uncomfortable.

"DS Monteith we want you to get close to Russell. You already have seen inside his casino so you're the best person to do this."

"You mean you don't want a scandal, and if I don't do this I am demoted or out of a job. You're nuts, you're putting a target on my back and hanging me out to dry." Monteith was starting to lose it.

"We will also pay off your five thousand pound gambling

debt and may be giving you some extra cash to help with your assignment. You can use it how you wish, but you need to report back to us what you have spent and what on. But if you get into trouble again with your gambling you're on your own. We will not bail you out AGAIN."

36

TUESDAY EVENING.

MONTEITH SAT IN HIS CAR, his mind was turning somersaults.

Each half of his brain felt like it was against the other in a WWE wrestling match, one fall, submission or a knockout. On the seat next to him was an envelope containing the five grand Matthews gave him to pay off Russell. Five grand which did not just come with strings attached but came with a hangman's noose. He had phoned ahead prior to leaving the station making sure he could see Russell.

Now here he was sat in front of the casino contemplating his next move.

Flight or fight.

The casino was almost empty with it being early evening as Monteith entered. The main trade, the high rollers, came in late evening spending enough to keep a small country out of debt. He was met by the same two bouncers who escorted him on his last visit. As they came out of the lift, the Russell brothers were deep in conversation and pointing as they looked over the balcony at the casino floor below.

"Mr. Monteith, please join us."

James Russell beckoned him over putting his arm around his shoulder as Monteith stood by him.

"We were discussing about making some changes. Adding some more things in, more fruit machines, another blackjack table. We are also thinking of adding a men only club in one of the rooms at the back. Maximising revenue streams, what do you think?"

"Err, I don't know. If you think you need to then go ahead," Monteith garbled.

"See Allan, even Mr Monteith here thinks it's a good idea." Russell said slapping Monteith on the back. "But discussing this is not why you're here."

Monteith dug around in his jacket before pulling out the envelope of money.

"It's all there, your five grand."

Russell took and opened it, smiling as he did it and looking like someone had returned five thousand of his children. He nodded to the bouncers who grabbed Monteith by the arms, holding him. Monteith struggled but could not get free.

"Thank you, Mr. Monteith, now that was not hard to do." Russell patted him on the cheek, demeaning him. "See Mr. Monteith to his car lads."

With that Russell walked off with his brother to his inner sanctum.

37

WEDNESDAY

THE MORTUARY WAS BEGINNING to feel like a second home to Watson and Monteith over the last few weeks.

They were there this morning for the autopsy of the body which was brought out of the river yesterday. Mac and his assistant were dressed in all their finery, green scrubs, yellow wellies and gloves, and masks which looked like they came from the local welders.

Both the detectives standing well back from the table were kitted out in the same gear except for the gloves and masks. They had paper masks on because the stench radiating from the body was bad even before it was cut open. It was too much for Monteith who emptied the contents of his stomach into a nearby sink before staggering out of the door his face the colour of his scrubs.

After cutting away the body's clothes and giving it a clean, Mac came across something of interest. He removed his mask.

"Watson, I think I found how he died."

Mac's assistant started taking photos of where he was pointing.

Watson approached the table his hand holding his mask

closer to his face trying to cut down on the smell. Mac pointed to two holes in the body's chest.

"Looks like he was shot before ending up in the river. I'll see if the bullets are still in there when I open him up."

"Was there any I.D. on him?"

"No, I will have to use his teeth for ID. His fingertips have been eaten by fish and other wildlife along with other parts of his body."

Mac showed the damaged fingers, ears and lips. The body moaned as trapped gases started to escape. Watson backed away from the table as the stench grew stronger.

"Jesus, that's rank. How can you work on a body like this?"

"Luckily, we don't get many bloaters, but you get used to it after a while. The fire victims are the worst. It takes forever to get the smell of smoke and burnt flesh out of here. The sales of air fresheners go up when we have one of them," Mac commented as if it was a normal occurrence.

"I will check the missing persons reports when I get back, somebody has to be wondering where he is, thanks Mac." Watson started going towards the door.

"Don't you want to stay for the examination?" Mac asked holding a scalpel. "I was just about to cut him open."

"Can I quote you? You only do the bodies; the rest is for us to work out."

LITTLEWOOD AND SUSAN WERE RELAXING AT THEIR WOODLAND retreat.

They sunbathed on the decking. Walked along the miles of woodland trails, even did a spot of swimming in the camp's indoor pool. Susan noticed she was being eyed up by some of the older boys who were trying to outdo each other posing around the sides of the pool. She was flattered by the attention, wishing it was at a different time and place. Her father had also noticed from where he sat.

He smiled to himself with pride, his daughter being the centre of attention for once.

She'd had a crap upbringing. He knew that. Helping a depressive alcoholic after her mother's murder was something no child should have to go through. But she had, and she was now blooming into a beautiful young woman.

"Why don't you go and enjoy yourself?" Littlewood suggested to Susan as she came back to the table.

"No! I came with you. We are on holiday together."

Susan was put out with her father.

"Listen, I will be all right. Tomorrow we have a big day. You need to let your hair down. You have been looking after me for years. It's time you did something for yourself."

"But Dad!"

"No buts," Littlewood put a hand on her arm and spoke softly.

"I've seen those boys over there looking at you. Go and talk to them, enjoy yourself. I will be fine." Susan leant over and kissed him on his forehead, "Thanks Dad."

When Watson and Monteith arrived back at the station, Monteith ran directly to the toilets.

Seeing the latest body at the morgue really affected him. Watson had to drive back in Monteith's car, stopped on the way because Monteith needed to be sick again.

"Where's Monteith?" Lorimer asked as Watson walked into the office.

He was at his computer with Crompton looking through the latest missing persons list. Watson had phoned through when he stopped for Monteith on the way back.

"Kermit's in the toilet groaning down the big white telephone. That last body really turned his stomach."

"Kermit?" Lorimer laughed out loud. "It was that bad?"

"Oh yes. Even I struggled but survived." Watson joined in with the laughing.

"I had better see how he is," Crompton sighed, got up and headed for the toilets.

"How are you doing with missing persons?" Watson asked as he was getting a drink.

"We have only just started. There's a few out there, but none at the moment match our body. We might have to wait until Mac has done his business."

Monteith was washing his face when Crompton entered.

"How are you Keith?" Monteith stood up and grabbed a handful of paper towels. "I'll be fine boss. Just give me ten minutes."

"No, looking at you I am ordering you to take the rest of the day off to recover."

"No, I'm fine."

"That's an order. You are not much good to me in the state you're in. Terry told me what happened so go home."

Crompton made sure he was not taking no again for an answer. Monteith nodded, and they both exited the toilet.

"Before you go, did you pay off Russell last night?" Crompton enquired.

"Yes, I paid him. He was discussing something with his brother when I got there. I didn't stay around too long before his goons threw me out."

"Did you catch what they were discussing?"

"Catch it? He told me! They are going to expand the casino. Bringing in a male only club." Monteith's face was quickly tuning from green to a lovely chalk white colour.

"Interesting, right you get off now. Don't come back to until the morning."

He escorted Monteith to the lift and sent him on his way.

Susan was enjoying her time away from her father.

She had seen him make his way back to the cabin some time ago. After changing out of her swimwear and into something she thought was less revealing, she walked around the holiday site taking everything in. They had been to other camps before, but that was when her mother was alive.

Susan felt alive, free even if it was only for a few hours.

38

THURSDAY

LITTLEWOOD AND SUSAN packed up their things and started their journey back into West Ravenswood.

With their rental 4x4 they could slip into the city hopefully un- noticed. They kept off the main roads to add to reduce the risk of not being seen. Nothing was said once they set off. That had been done in the cabin. They had worked out what needed to be done and how it was to be carried out. It was a bit like going into the lion's den. Would the police be there? Would they be able to get McNulty and Smith without raising suspicion? Would they bump into someone from Claythorn who recognised them?

They had come this far and none of that would put them off.

Littlewood pulled into the visitor's car park, parking close enough so if everything went to plan they could be in and out quickly. Littlewood looked at Susan and smiled.

"Thank you for everything."

A tear rolled down his cheek.

"We are family and family comes first." Susan wiped the tear away and kissed him on the cheek. With that she got out and waited for the prison doors to open.

The pickup was easier than they both thought it would go. Smith and McNulty came like lambs to the slaughter. Well, they were not given a chance of doing anything else, with Susan sticking a gun in the ribs of McNulty and telling them if they did anything stupid they would be killed on the spot. When they got into the back seat of the 4x4 their hands were bound with Ty-wraps and told not to make any sudden moves alerting anyone or they would be shot immediately.

Littlewood drove out of the car park normally, trying to not attract attention from other released inmates and their families. Susan was in the back, making sure nothing happened.

They headed for wasteland and disused buildings on the edge of the city. A brownfield area which was down for redevelopment, but nothing had been started yet due to council planning dragging their heels. Littlewood pulled into the derelict warehouse and parked up. McNulty and Smith had become agitated on the drive over, but thankfully for all of them they tried nothing in the way of causing trouble.

Littlewood pulled McNulty out of the 4x4; Susan, brandishing the gun, got Smith out of the other side. They made them kneel next to each other in the dirt and rubbish on the floor.

"Let me introduce myself. My name is Colin Littlewood, and you murdered my wife and Susan's mother."

"But we didn't," McNulty struggled to say.

"Shut up. I don't want to hear your snivelling or pity. It won't help where you are going."

"She fell, we didn't touch her." Smith shouted. Susan pointed the gun at him.

"Did you not hear my father, shut up."

"You were still in our house, you were robbing us. If you were not in our house, she would not have died. YOU KILLED MY WIFE."

His face was just inches away from Smith's, looking straight into the frightened man's eyes.

Smith turned his face away. Littlewood raged with anger and punched him twice in the face. Smith howled in pain as his nose dripped blood.

McNulty didn't miss out as Littlewood kicked him in the stomach making him keel over sideways. With McNulty coughing and gasping, Littlewood dragged him back up to a kneeling position and unloaded a couple of punches to his face.

Susan looked at her father standing there with hatred in his eyes. She understood the anger he was feeling, and it had to be released.

"You're a nutter, a lunatic; you're the one that should be locked up," Smith shouted.

For that outburst he got a kick in the stomach, followed by a flurry of punches to the face. Smith tried to cover up but to no avail. Littlewood grabbed him by the hair and pulled him up.

Susan was getting worried. She had never seen her father like this before.

"Dad!"

He looked at her with a glazed over look in his eyes and puffing hard, trying to get his breath back.

"Dad, can we finish this?" She handed over the gun. "Let's get out of here."

Littlewood looked down at the weapon and then at McNulty and Smith. Both were staring back at him, shouting at him but he could not hear them. He was in a world of his own. He stepped forward and placed the gun on McNulty's forehead. McNulty was screaming. Littlewood pulled the gun away and placed it on Smith's forehead causing Smith to try to pull away. Littlewood hit him on the head with the gun for that. Blood rolling down from the gash it made.

"Dad, shoot them."

Susan did not like what she was seeing. When working this out they had decided to just shoot them and disappear. What she saw in her father's actions was starting to scare her. Littlewood looked at Susan with a smile on his face.

"No, we are not going to kill them here. Shootings too good for them. I have a better idea."

"What you talking about Dad? We had it all sorted?"

"Get them back into the 4x4, we are going for a little drive."

"Where? Tell me Dad? I'm getting worried."

"The multi-storey. Chucking them off the top of there seems a fitting end for them considering."

"But Dad?"

Littlewood shot a look at her.

"You not behind me anymore? Remember, family comes first. That's what you are always saying."

"Yes, I am always with you. It's just we had a plan, now you want to change it?"

"Right get them in the car and you're driving." He threw the keys at her signalling the end of the discussion.

McNulty and Smith were bungled into the back of the 4x4, lying on the floor so no-one could see them. Littlewood put masking tape over their mouths, mainly to stop them whining.

A couple more swift punches to each of them added to the "Do not move or else" threat.

Susan pulled out of the warehouse and started back

into the city. Littlewood was in the passenger seat, gun on his lap.

She didn't know what to make of her father. He had done a complete U-turn in the way he was acting. From alcoholic and depressive-looking, to sounding like a man in control.

In control of what?

Maybe this horror was coming to an end, he did not care about anything. Fearing that it included her, she looked at him, he was calm. As if out for a Sunday drive. There were little signs he could blow at any time. The manic look in his eyes. His legs twitching., always glancing over his shoulder at their captives. Fingering the trigger on the gun, stroking it like a pet.

Then it all went off.

They pulled up to a set of traffic lights. Beside them a police car drew up. One officer looked across and nudged his partner, who also looked and nodded. Littlewood smiled at the officers and wound down his window. Before they could react, Littlewood fired at the car taking out the windscreen.

"DRIVE, DRIVE, DRIVE!" he shouted at Susan, who shaking with fear slammed it into gear and floored it.

Wheels screeching the 4x4 launched forward into traffic. Susan managed not to hit anything as they took off down the road like a scalded cat.

"What the hell did you do that for?" Susan shouted back at her father.

"They'd recognised us."

"But you did not have to shoot at them for Christ sake."

Susan was looking in her rear-view mirror checking they were not following them.

"Shut up and get us to the multi-storey."

39

EVERYONE in the office stopped what they were doing when Crompton threw down his phone.

He jumped out of his chair turning the air blue with expletives, slamming both his fists hard onto his desk. Storming out of his office, the door nearly coming off its hinges as he grabbed it.

"They were released this morning," Crompton shouted across the room. His face red with rage. "They fucking released McNulty and Smith this morning!"

"What do you mean they were released this morning? We were told it would be tomorrow," Monteith replied nearly spilling his coffee.

"I've just got off the phone with the governor and they released McNulty and Smith at 8am."

Watson looked at his watch, 9.30am.

"They could be anywhere by now," Watson said with frustration. "Who picked them up? Their families?"

"Don't have a clue. The governor did not know. Once they are out of their front gates, they are not the prison's problem." Crompton was fuming. "I have told him we wanted to see their CCTV coverage of their front gate as soon as possible. If not, I will be charging him with obstruction of a police investigation. I am going there straight away. Watson, Monteith you are coming with me. At least you can stop me from hitting him."

By the time they had arrived at Claythorn twenty minutes later, Crompton's anger had not subsided. He stormed up to the main door, leaving Watson and Monteith in his wake.

"Boss, Boss, calm down." Watson was trying to keep up. "They'll not let you see anyone if you go in like Storming Norman, wanting things done. This is not your territory, and you cannot go and throw your weight around."

"I know, but they have just released two men possibly into the arms of a waiting psycho. What the hell were they doing?"

"Their job," Watson replied. "Right when we go in just stand back and compose yourself. I'll book us in at reception."

Watson approached the reception desk and introduced himself to one of the security officers behind the security glass.

"DCI Crompton, DS Watson and DS Monteith to see Governor Greenslade. We are expected."

Looking up he saw the CCTV cameras which were both inside and outside the main door. Both Crompton and Monteith showed their ID to the officer.

They were escorted upstairs and into a side office and asked to wait. The office was fitted out with CCTV monitors and recording equipment. Two officers sat in front of the bank of equipment. The screens showed every part of the prison they could. They stood there and watched the daily routine and ritual of prison life.

"Where is he?" Crompton mumbled under his breath.

"Be patient." Watson knew his boss was still on a short fuse.

The door opened and in strode Governor Greenslade with

a blue manila coloured folder in his hand. He looked like a headmaster of old. Greying hair, rounded metal glasses, shirt and tie jumper and checked jacket.

"Sorry to keep you waiting gentlemen, my P.A. suddenly rang in saying she was taking a few days off and I have had trouble finding the relevant paperwork. I have had to rearrange an important meeting because of this. Have we got the CCTV footage from this morning?" He asked one of the officers.

"Yes Sir, it's all set up."

"Who was it you were interested in DCI?" Greenslade acted as if he could not be bothered with it all.

"Mr. Greenslade," Crompton said through gritted teeth.

"I am sorry we have ruined your morning, but we believe two of your former lodgers are in danger. And we would like to find out why they were released twenty-four hours before the date we were told, and who picked them up. Now if it's not too much trouble, we would like to see the footage and have a very good explanation of what the hell went on."

By the time he had stopped talking his voice has gone up three octaves and he was so close to Greenslade, he could count the hairs in his nose.

"Right, ok, mmm, run the tape Craig," Greenslade said.

The first clip was of fourteen people milling inside the reception area, ready to be called forward to the main gate. Some stood talking to each other. Others paced around eager to be released.

"Which ones are McNulty and Smith?" Monteith asked.

"They're the ones at the back," the officer named Craig said, pointing them out.

They were not talking to anyone, keeping themselves to themselves.

"Do inmates get released every day?" Monteith was intrigued.

"Yes except for weekends and bank holidays. If their release date falls on one of those days, they go on a Friday."

"Is there a limit to the number you release at the same time?"

"No, if it's your time you go. Could be one that day, could be fifty"

Monteith looked closer at the prisoners being released now. "Hey Terry, have a look at this. Isn't that Justin Taylor?" Watson joined him and looked at the man that

Monteith was pointing to.

"Yes, my God! Didn't we put him away for those jewellery raids five years ago? And look there's Darren Barnes. He was done for glassing that bloke in the Carpenters Arms. GBH wasn't it after the bloke lost an eye in the attack."

"When you two have stopped playing guess the crime, looks like they are on the way out, now concentrate," Crompton admonished.

The inmates were walking out of the reception and to the large metal front gate. Time on the tape read 8 am. McNulty and Smith keeping their distance at the back. The tape switched to outside the gate. Relatives gathered waiting for their loved ones to be released after their incarceration for whatever they had done. A line of taxis were parked if needed.

The gate slid back on its rollers with lights and a siren sounding. Even before it got half way they poured out, running to their waiting loved ones. Some disappeared for the walk into town to catch the next bus or train out of the city.

"Where are McNulty and Smith?" Crompton wanted to know.

"They have just come out, bottom left of the screen," Watson pointed out.

"Don't lose them."

They turned to walk towards the city centre. As the got

close to the visitor's car park, a lady approached them and looked like she was talking to them.

"Who is that woman talking to them? Does anybody know?" Crompton was getting wound up again.

"That's Susan Farmer, my P.A.," Greenslade suddenly said his voice filled with shock.

They all turned to look at him.

"That is your P.A?" Crompton was confused.

"Yes. She rang in yesterday, saying she was taking a few days way with her father because he was not well."

"Well, it looks like she's not gone anywhere to me." Crompton snapped back. "How does she know McNulty and Smith?"

"I don't know."

"Look at this?" Watson had kept watching the tape.

Susan was now escorting them towards a car. "She's got them at bloody gunpoint."

She made them get into the back of a 4x4 still holding the gun. A man in the driver's seat turned to speak to McNulty and Smith.

"Is there another CCTV we can see of the visitors' car park, so we can see what went on?"

"I'll check," the officer called Craig said.

Crompton let rip at the governor.

"Right Mr. Greenslade, how the hell did they get released twenty-four hours before they should have? Any ideas please because I'm damned if I'm leaving this after what I've just seen."

40

"I have CCTV from the visitors' car park," Craig shouted above the commotion.

The first showed McNulty and Smith walking towards Susan. As they reached her, she pulled the gun out and said something to them. She stuck the gun into the side of McNulty making sure they knew she was not messing around.

They walked towards the visitors' car park.

"Didn't anyone see this happen at the time?" Monteith said quizzically.

Both the officers on the CCTV equipment shook their heads.

As they reached a 4x4, the driver got out.

"That's Littlewood!" Watson exclaimed. "Shit, they've got McNulty and Smith."

"That must be his daughter." Monteith stood not wanting to believe what he was seeing.

They shoved McNulty and Smith into the back. Words were exchanged, and it looked like the gun was waved in their faces as a warning. The 4x4 soon left the car park heading toward the city centre.

Monteith and Watson stood looking at each other not wanting to say what they were thinking. Crompton broke the silence with exactly what he was thinking.

"Well, that was one big fuck up we have just seen. And Greenslade I am looking at the biggest fuck up here. This is your entire fault. How two inmates are released 24 hours before their due release date? I want to see the paperwork. If anything happens to them I am holding you responsible."

Greenslade handed over the folder he had been holding. "All the details are in there."

Watson's phone ring out, and he went out of the room to take it.

Crompton opened it and started reading. According to the official printout from the prison's records, McNulty and Smith were to have been released tomorrow. But the copy of the release letter that was given to them gave a date of today.

"Who writes out these letters?" Crompton waved them at Greenslade.

"Susan, my P.A. - once I've seen and confirmed the details of the Parole Board."

"And you don't check them before they go out?"

"No, I've no need to. I trust Susan."

Before Crompton could lose his temper again with Greenslade, Watson came flying back into the room.

"That was the station. We have sight of Littlewoods's car. It's in the multi-storey, top level.

"Any sighting of them," Monteith asked.

"They're unsure if they are in the car, uniform is keeping their distance a level below. Armed response has been called."

It took time for them to get out of the prison, with having to get through all the security. That made Crompton's frustration even worse. He sat in the back of Monteith's BMW cursing and swearing at anything and everything. They received a police squad car escort to get them through the traffic for the final mile. The roads around the multi-storey had been closed off. The police had this down to a tee seeing as the multi-storey was a favourite place for the desperate and the despondent to end their lives by jumping off it.

They pulled up by the entrance. Lorimer jumped into the back.

"What's happening?" Crompton asked still stressed out.

"Littlewood's car was spotted about twenty minutes ago by a vigilant PC and was pursued. Two squad cars attempted to stop him. Shots were fired by the people in Littlewood's car at our squad cars. One was hit shattering the windscreen. Luckily no officer was hit. The other car followed him to this car park, and up onto the top level. Littlewood is parked at one end, and the squad car is at the other. They have not approached the car, and as far as I am aware no one has got out of it yet. The car park has been cleared up to the level below. And cars still on that and the top the owners are being kept together away from the area, but close enough to get them when it's clear. Armed response has arrived and is on the level below along with the hostage negotiator."

Lorimer's run down was thorough. They could hear the police helicopter flying over.

"Where is Matthews?" Crompton asked.

"Still back at headquarters but wanting to be kept updated."

"Good. Don't want him around bungling this up. Right let's get up there."

Monteith was let through the police cordon at the entrance. Driving slowly up the ramps of the car park onto the deserted levels was very eerie. Normally they would be full of the cars of shoppers and workers from the nearby offices, who had paid for weekly or monthly passes. Moving up onto the sixth level, they pulled over and met up with the head of the armed response unit.

They were handed flak jackets in case anything went off.

"The car has been static for about 10 minutes. Looks like

four people in the car. Not much movement in the back, but the two in the front have been animated in conversation," The ARU officer advised.

"Can we get any closer?" Crompton asked.

"Yes, but we need to be cautious."

There was a cracking voice over his radio.

"Movement at the car, repeat movement at the car, doors being opened."

"Anybody getting out?"

"Two in front out first. Opening back doors, two people in back being dragged out of car. Looks like they are bound up."

The ARU officer turned to Crompton,

"You wanted to get closer. Let's move up, it's getting interesting."

The ARU slowly went up the last ramp onto the top level. They spaced out using cars which had been trapped up there as cover. Firearms had been drawn.

Crompton, Watson, Monteith and Lorimer came up behind and were told to stay back for the time being.

Littlewood and his daughter had got out of the car and were standing by the outside wall.

Below them, the road leading to the car park. Deserted of traffic. Emergency vehicles waiting in case they were needed.

Between them were McNulty and Smith. They had tape across their mouths, and their wrists were bound with Ty-wraps behind their backs. They looked like they had been beaten. Their faces were swollen, and blood had dripped down on to their clothes. The frightened look in their eyes was all too evident.

The Littlewoods were arguing so much they did not seem to notice the AFU. If they had noticed them they were not going to let them put off what they were doing. It was not until the hostage negotiator used the loudhailer that they reacted.

"Colin, Susan. This is the West Ravenswood police. Please

put down your weapons and release your hostages." No response came back. They both looked at the police at the other end of the level. Some had moved closer behind parked cars.

"Colin, please think of what you're doing. What do you require so we can end this?"

"JUSTICE, JUSTICE FOR MY WIFE," Littlewood shouted. "For these two miserable cowards, to pay for what they did."

Crompton grabbed the loudhailer.

"Littlewood give it up. You cannot get out of this. They paid for what they did, in prison. Put your weapons down and release them."

"NO, NO, NO, I'M NOT."

With that he pushed Smith to the edge. Smith's top half of his body leaning over it. Smith screamed out, seeing his life flash before his eyes.

"DAD NO," Susan suddenly blurted out. "I am not being a part of this. We had an agreement. I have had enough."

Susan ran towards the police shouting

"HELP, DON'T SHOOT. I WANT TO GIVE UP."

"Stop right there," one of the AFU officers ordered. "Down on the floor, hands on your head."

Susan stopped straight away. She got down on her knees, then flat out on her front. As soon as she did that four AFU officers moved forward. They surrounded her while she was being cuffed.

A burst of gunfire caught everybody off guard.

"Who fired? Who fired?" The head of the AFU shouted. "No order was given."

Everyone looked around, wondering who it was. "Boss? What the hell are you doing?"

Watson was staring at Crompton. He was standing with his gun pulled at arm's length.

"Terry, look!"

Monteith was pointing past where Susan and the AFU

officers were. Colin Littlewood was lying on the floor. McNulty and Smith were crouched by the wall trying to get as far away as possible. A small group of AFU officers were making their way over to Littlewood slowly covering each other. One checked Littlewood, feeling for a pulse. Three gunshot wounds were visible, one in the head and two in the body. The officer confirmed over the radio that Littlewood was dead.

"Boss, give me your gun." Watson spoke slowly to Crompton.

"Boss, please."

Crompton turned his head towards Watson. His eyes were glazed over.

"He wanted justice. I have just given it to him." Crompton said with a harsh tone of voice. "And justice for Elizabeth Preston."

"Boss: your gun, and don't say anything else."

Crompton slowly nodded and let Watson take his gun.

"DCI Crompton, I am arresting you. You do not have to say anything. But, it may harm your defence if you do not mention when questioned something which you later rely on in court. Anything you do say may be given in evidence."

"Do we have to read him his rights?" Monteith whispered.

Watson thought. "It's best if we do."

Monteith guided Crompton back to a waiting squad car after putting the handcuffs on. Everyone was in silence watching as the car set off for the headquarters. Watson had handed Crompton's firearm to an AFU officer for investigation purposes.

It was put into a clear evidence bag and tagged.

41

Nobody felt like celebrating when they got back to the headquarters.

Yes, they had got a serial killer off the streets, but not in the way they wanted or begin to comprehend.

DCI Crompton was booked in down in the cells. Watson, Monteith and Lorimer had the ignominy of seeing their boss having his name taken the records, and why he was arrested. Having his mug shot and fingerprints taken. Having to watch as his personal items, belt, shoelaces and his uniform were taken from him and bagged in a large paper bag. And then, finally, being escorted down along to the cells, dressed in a paper boiler suit, and the door being banged shut behind him.

The next few days were taken up with paperwork, lots of it. The Independent Police Enquiry team was brought in to oversee everything. They interviewed Watson, Monteith and Lorimer for their versions of the events leading up to the killing of Colin Littlewood. Crompton had been taken to a police station well out of West Ravenswood jurisdiction for his interview and his arraignment. The interviews were a waste of time as the only thing Crompton said throughout was "NO COMMENT."

SUSAN LITTLEWOOD, ONCE SHE WAS RELEASED FROM HOSPITAL and into police custody, told them her father made her do everything.

She was frightened of him and went along with what he wanted from getting the job at the prison to helping compile the list in the red book, which the forensic officers found while searching the Littlewoods' home. Family now did not come first.

Now she was on her own.

The list contained seventeen names in all, four of which had been crossed out. As Watson and Monteith scanned the list, two names popped out, those of Billy and Joseph Clayton. How close had they been to being the next victims?

The Criminal Detective Agency needed a new leader. Watson and Monteith had been there the longest, but they knew Matthews would bring in someone from another area. Watson had been a stand in until a new boss was installed. Rumours had been doing the rounds about who it could be.

That happened the next week. Watson, Monteith and Lorimer were going through cases they were working on when a smiling Matthews walked into the office. Behind him was a smartly dressed lady in a black pant suit with a cream blouse, carrying a briefcase. She stood by him as he called the office to order.

"Gentlemen if I can have your attention. I would like to introduce the new boss of the Criminal Detective Agency, DCI Tanya Wright."

"Good afternoon detectives." Tanya introduced herself,

but Matthews directed her to the now cleared office of DCI Crompton and shut the door.

"Now that, I was not expecting."

Monteith stood up and gestured towards the office.

"What, Matthews being kind or the new DCI?" Watson asked.

"Both."

Matthews came out of the office and walked straight past them without looking at them. DCI Wright stood in the office doorway.

"Gentlemen, if you would step this way. It's time for some introductions."

42

A MONTH LATER

MONTEITH WAS glad his day had finished.

Superintendent Matthews had been pressing him again to get information on the Russell's, but he was getting nowhere with just being a patron of the casino. They kept their business and private lives separate. Trying to make a jerk like Matthews understand that was impossible.

The serial killer Littlewood had been killed.

His daughter had been locked up awaiting trial for murder, kidnapping, aiding and abetting and anything else they could throw at her. She confirmed during interview that her father killed Duncan Healey. Crompton was facing disgrace and a court trial for his murder of Littlewood. DCI Tanya Wright had taken over and was still getting her feet under the table.

Watson had gone into town to meet his wife and children for a meal. Monteith, at least he could relax at least for a couple of days before re-entering the madhouse that was the Criminal Detective Agency.

Walking towards his BMW Series 1, he flicked through the messages that had been left on his iPhone. Just the normal crap he thought. As he approached his car, two men dressed in dark clothing suddenly appeared in front of him. One of them smashed a right-handed punch into Monteith's face. He went down like the proverbial sack of spuds, bouncing of the front off the car next to him. Before he knew it, a hessian bag was forced over his head and his hands were bound behind his back with Ty-wraps.

"What the hell, who are you?"

Monteith shouted, feeling the full force of a kick in the stomach knocking the wind out of his lungs. He heard a van pull up next to him and doors opening. Whoever it was who attacked him, lifted him off the floor and threw him into the back of the van. Doors were slammed shut, and the engine revved as the van moved off.

Allan Russell watched the unfolding event from his car at a safe distance. The boss's boys were doing their job down to the letter. It looked like Monteith did not know what hit him as the boys grabbed him and stuffed him into the van. He waited till the van has cleared the car park before he followed at a safe distance.

"Got you," he said to himself.

Jimmy Russell was sampling one of the finest scotches in his collection, a Highland Park 32-year-old, distilled in 1974, and bottled in 2006. Only one hundred and forty-one bottles were made.

As he leant back in his leather chair, his phone rang out on the desk. It was a text message.

"Your package has been collected."

ACKNOWLEDGMENTS

My wife Ann, who gave me the push to write this book, instead of having it only in my head.

Ross Greenwood who let me bounce ideas off him and let me pick his brains over parts of the book.

All the other authors on Facebook who I have spoken to and taken on board what they have said. KA Richardson, Tara Lyons, David Evans to name a few.

Kathryn Bax and everyone connected to the One Stop Fiction Authors Resource Group on Facebook.

David McCaffrey and everyone at BNBS for their backing.

And finally, Julie Timlin, whose guidance and comments were invaluable and so very appreciated.

Thank You.

ABOUT THE AUTHOR

Tony was born in Warrington Cheshire in 1967, but moved to Rutland in 1981 with his family.

Attending Uppingham Community College, Rutland sixth form and later attending Stamford College.

He has done various jobs, including a lifeguard, white van man, and temp work but working at RAF Wyton as a civil servant for the MOD for many years was his most loved career, sadly ending in redundancy due to all the cuts to the civil service.

He married his wife in 1996 and his son was born a year later. They live in Cambridgeshire, UK. with two mad cats. His son attending University at present.

Tony has always wanted to write a book and this is his first, deciding he really needed to do it as he had time on his hands.

He is working on the next.

Printed in Poland
by Amazon Fulfillment
Poland Sp. z o.o., Wrocław